"Do you have a problem working for a woman, Mr. Steele?"

"It's Hardt. Steele Hardt."

Surely he was making that up. "Is that what it says on your birth certificate?"

His smile was almost as breath-robbing as his eyes. Every survival instinct she possessed screamed "danger."

"My mother has a warped sense of humor. And no, I have never had problems taking direction from a woman."

Montana suddenly grew warm, perspiration dewing her hairline, and she felt a surge of blood, like an adrenaline rush. His words sounded innocent enough, so why did she read sexual overtones into them? It must've been his voice, the way it feathered her nerve endings with promises. Or was it the way his eyes suggested he welcomed a woman's guidance in pleasuring her to the utmost?

"Good. I run Black Creek. I'm the one you'll be answering to."

His smile widened. "I can't wait."

A HARD MAN TO LOVE

A Hard Man to Love is also available as an eBook

UNTAMED

"Full of wit and charm . . . highly entertaining. Full of adventure, romance, and daring-do . . . imagine Nancy Drew meets *Sex and the City*!"

—*Roundtable Reviews*

"Kathleen Lawless' story is fresh. . . . The dialogue is snappy and unique and the sex is riveting."

—*Romance Junkies*

"The growing relationship between the fully developed lead couple makes for a wonderful, heated tale."

—Harriet Klausner, *The Best Reviews*

UNMASKED

"Passionate and erotic. . . . Readers looking for steamy, sensual scenes will love it."

—*Roundtable Reviews*

"Lawless weaves romance, intrigue, and excitement into an impressive tapestry. Do not miss this book."

—*Romance Reviews Today*

"An amusing, spirited, adventurous tale."

—*Romantic Times*

"A sensual read that will keep you spellbound until the very end."

—*Romance Junkies*

TABOO

"An engaging erotic romance . . . an entertaining tale."

—*Midwest Book Review*

". . . filled with erotic interludes."

—*A Romance Review*

All available from Pocket Books

Also by Kathleen Lawless

Untamed

Unmasked

Taboo

A Hard Man to Love

Kathleen Lawless

POCKET BOOKS
New York London Toronto Sydney

POCKET BOOKS, a division of Simon & Schuster, Inc.
1230 Avenue of the Americas, New York, NY 10020

This book is a work of fiction. Names, characters, places, and incidents are products of the author's imagination or are used fictitiously. Any resemblance to actual events or locales or persons, living or dead, is entirely coincidental.

ISBN-13: 978-1-4165-0752-9
ISBN-10: 1-4165-0752-3

This Pocket Books trade paperback edition August 2006

10 9 8 7 6 5 4 3 2 1

Manufactured in the United States of America

For information regarding special discounts for bulk purchases, please contact Simon & Schuster Special Sales at 1-800-456-6798 or business@simonandschuster.com.

Dedicated to my dear friend Gina, who underwent brain surgery with exceptional courage and grace, as I wrote this book.

Acknowledgments

Many people deserve thanks for their help with this project. Among them: The Le Sage family, who introduced me to Las Vegas, and Doug Taylor, who shared the world of the professional gambler. Diane and Barry, for the fun at the Grotto Spa. Pamela, my equestrian expert, along with the PMA babes for their selfless assistance researching spa treatments. Pilot Jason Stewart, who shared his flying expertise and passion, and Larry Michaels, who mapped out flight routes and times.

Sincere apologies to anyone I left out. Do know that I appreciate you all. What would a girl do without her friends?

Chapter One

"Helen, this time you've really gone too far." Montana Blackstone eyed her mother-in-law, perched daintily across the desk. What in the world was she going to do with her?

"Montana, darling, give the man a chance, won't you?"

"You cannot sleep with every man on this ranch who takes your fancy, then fire them when they no longer suit your needs!"

Helen's surgically rejuvenated face flushed pink. "You're exaggerating."

"Not by much." Montana would have liked to add that if Charlie was still alive he'd be appalled by his mother's behavior, but the truth of it was they were cut from the same cloth, these two. Charlie had also slept with the help, then fired them when he was done.

"I know Steele will be a tremendous asset to Black Creek. He's a lucky find. You've been so immersed in the resort and spa, you have no idea how the rest of the ranch is faring."

"I know it hasn't been our best season," Montana admitted.

"It needs an infusion of fresh ideas and energy," Helen said. "You can't continue your expansion without the revenue."

"It's nearly done," Montana said.

"And over budget," Helen said, a fact Montana couldn't dispute. The state-of-the-art spa had spiraled out of control with delays and cost overruns, and what had started out as an exciting new project was rapidly turning into a mess of red ink.

Helen's decision to hire a new foreman wasn't really Montana's to override, for although Helen didn't control the purse strings, she did have the ear of Black Creek Resort's guarantor.

"All right, then. Let's go meet your latest boy toy and get it over with."

"For the record, he's not my type."

When Montana saw him, she had to agree. Just the way the man stood in the tiled entrance hall of the ranch house, his back toward them, his Stetson loosely clasped between his fingers, screamed power and control and capability. He was studying a painting by Lamotia, one of Montana's favorite artists, and she had a brief moment to take in his thick dark hair and broad shoulders before the newcomer turned to face them. She caught her breath, speared by the most intensely blue eyes she had ever seen. Somewhere between genuine turquoise and desert night sky, they were breathtaking, mesmerizing, rendering her temporarily speechless.

"Steele, Montana, I'll leave you two to chat." With a smug smile, Helen retreated.

"Sorry," the stranger said. "I didn't mean to stare, but I expected Montana to be a man."

His remark restored her equilibrium as effectively as a dash of cold water. "Do you have a problem working for a woman, Mr. Steele?"

"It's Hardt."

"I beg your pardon."

"Steele Hardt."

Surely he was making that up. "Is that what it says on your birth certificate?"

His smile was almost as breath-robbing as his eyes. Every survival instinct she possessed screamed "danger."

"My mother has a warped sense of humor, but I always figure it could have been worse: my brother's name is Sloan. And no, I have never had problems taking direction from a woman."

Despite the silent overhead fan stirring the air, Montana felt herself grow suddenly warm. Beads of perspiration dewed her hairline while nerve sensors went on full alert. She felt a surge of blood through her system, like an adrenaline rush. His words sounded innocent enough; so why did she read sexual overtones into them? It must've been his voice, the way it feathered her nerve endings with promise. Or was it his eyes, and the way they suggested he welcomed a woman's guidance in pleasuring her to the utmost?

"Despite what Helen might have led you to believe, I run Black Creek. I'm the one you'll be answering to."

He tilted his head in acknowledgment. "I can't wait."

"And sleeping with Helen is not part of your job description."

His smile widened. "That's a relief."

"Because once she sleeps with someone, one of us ends up firing him. So be warned."

"Sounds like danger pay could be in order," he said lightly.

Montana smiled in spite of herself. It was impossible not to, when his smile was contagious. "I hadn't planned to hire a new foreman, but Helen's right. Zeb's not getting any younger and my energies have been concentrated in other areas lately."

"Tell me, which one of you do they call the black widow?"

She slanted him a speculative glance. It was hard to know if he was being playful or provocative. Either way, Steele's presence at Black Creek would clearly be anything but dull.

"I have no idea. I imagine it depends whom you're speaking with. How did you convince Helen to hire you?"

"I come highly recommended."

"That's what I was afraid of," Montana said dryly. She extended her right hand. "Welcome to Black Creek, Mr. Hardt. I'll have Zeb show you to the bunkhouse and give you the lay of the land. Meet me back here after lunch."

Was it her imagination or did he clasp her hand a little longer than necessary? She swore she felt his thumb graze the sensitive area between thumb and forefinger, with the definite intent of turning it into an erogenous zone all its own.

"Meet you in this exact spot?"

She reclaimed her hand, which retained the warmth of his. "In my office. Second door on your left down that hall. We can fill out the necessary paperwork at that time."

"Before you hear my input?"

"Why would you offer your input before you're signed and sealed on the dotted line?"

"We shook hands," he said.

"Yes." And she still felt the warmth of his touch on her skin.

"Which is as binding to me as anything on paper. Any chance you can give me the guided tour in person?"

Montana took her time to answer, aware he was testing her, charting his boundaries; it was important she set the right tone. Steele seemed more the independent type than the order taker, exactly the kind of leadership the ranch needed, a change of pace from "good-time Charlie."

Her late husband had never been one to take control or deal with anything remotely unpleasant, yet she had a feeling that rather than back down from a challenge, Steele would welcome it with a challenge of his own. Perhaps she could learn to like having a capable man around the property for a change.

"I must say I'm not in the habit of rearranging my day at the whim of the newly hired help."

"If the old way of doing things was working, you'd hardly be in a position where you need me."

He was doing it again. Coloring seemingly innocent words with overtones of a sexual nature. Intimating she had need of individual services he was more than capable of providing.

"I don't need anyone," she said quickly, words that sounded forced, even to her.

"I used to think that, too. Then one day I learned differently."

She was dying to ask him what he meant by that cryptic statement but he changed subjects abruptly.

"What's going on with the spa?"

"I suggest you focus your energies in the direction of the ranch. The spa is none of your concern."

"I only asked a simple question," Steele said. "You needn't be so quick on the defensive."

"I would prefer for you to concentrate on matters that pertain directly to your ranching duties." As they spoke, they reached the massive, carved-on-both-sides front door of the ranch house.

Steele ushered her through ahead of him. "Whatever you say, Montana. Is it all right if I call you Montana? Both you and Helen are Mrs. Blackstone; it could get somewhat confusing."

"I hardly think people are likely to mix us up."

Outside, he wrenched open the passenger side of a dusty black pickup truck. "Hop in. You can direct me."

She climbed in, aware that although she'd never actually

agreed to accompany him, he seemed to accept it as fact, a skill that could make him a highly effective foreman.

The interior of the late model truck's cab was very clean, with nothing to give away hints regarding the personality of the vehicle's owner.

"Other than my office, I try to keep my home separate from the day-to-day operation of the ranch. Over there are the stables, bunkhouses, and guest cabins."

"Housing staff, or guests?"

"Both," she said. "Charlie, my late husband, believed the guests liked to be as close to the real action as possible."

The bunkhouses were looking a little run-down, she realized, viewing them with a critical eye as Steele pulled up around back. When had that happened? Was that why they had slowly been losing their regulars? Guests who returned at the same time year after year had become less common over the past few years, even before Charlie's death.

Steele parked around back of the first bunkhouse. "Where to from here, Boss Lady?"

His words made Montana realize just how long it had been since she'd shown her face anyplace other than the ranch house and the resort. She was saved from having to answer by the appearance of a grizzled ranch hand who eyed the new vehicle suspiciously.

"Knew that was a motor I didn't recognize." He turned to Montana. "Aren't you supposed to be on your way to the airport to pick up Fancy-Pants from California?"

"Oh, my word, I totally forgot. Zeb, this is Steele Hardt, who's going to be giving us a hand around here. Show him the lay of the land, would you? Steele, Zeb has been here longer than any of us can remember. He knows everything there is to know about Black Creek."

Zeb pulled her aside, out of earshot of Steele. "Didn't know you were fixing to take on anyone new."

"Neither did I. Helen hired him."

His expression darkened. "Mrs. Helen tends to forget her place."

"Yes, Helen and I have had that conversation. Would you do me a favor and show Steele around, please."

She raised her voice to address Steele. "I'll leave you in Zeb's capable hands, Mr. Hardt."

Montana drove as fast as she dared to the Medford Airport. It wouldn't make much of an impression on her new spa director if she left him stranded at the terminal. He was a fussy little man, a trait she'd discovered when she'd flown to L.A. to meet with him and lure him away from his position. At the time, fussy had struck her as just what she needed at the helm of the Oasis, for she tended to be a little too seat-of-her-pants in style.

She could try to blame Steele for distracting her this morning, but the truth was she'd been doing a damn fine job of distracting herself before he showed up, daydreaming into the future, when Black Creek Resort and Spa would be a world-class destination and household name.

She pulled up outside the arrivals area, relieved when Terence was not pacing outside the airport terminal, impatiently waiting for her. Perhaps his flight had been delayed. She pulled out her cell phone, which she had forgotten to turn on, and checked her messages. Next she called Terence's cell.

"Terence, Montana here. I'm out in front of the terminal. Where are you? . . . Still in L.A.? . . . But I don't understand . . . No, I haven't read my e-mail, I've been busy . . . I see . . . Well, I have to say I'm extremely disappointed . . . I understood we had reached an agreement.

"Unprofessional jerk," she muttered as she flipped the phone shut and pulled into the lane of traffic leaving the airport. Having the spa director quit before he'd even started was one more problem she really didn't need right now.

To find Steele lounging in her office upon her return was another. Never mind the fact that he was sitting behind her desk, with his booted feet propped on a corner of the desktop, the spa contractor's report in hand.

"You made good time to the airport and back."

"Just what do you think you're doing?" She stared with hard disapproval to where his feet rested on the desk she'd inherited from Charlie, along with the ranch and its responsibilities. She was determined to build on the legacy he had left, unsure if it was something she needed to prove more to herself or her dead husband's memory. Incensed, she gave Steele's feet a push designed to unbalance him, but he caught his footing and rose gracefully.

"You told me to meet you here. I know how long the airport drive takes, so I hurried through my tour to meet you when you got back." He glanced behind her. "Where's Fancy-Pants? Stand you up?"

"As a matter of fact, yes."

"Can't trust those city slickers." Steele clicked his tongue.

Any more than she could trust herself, Montana thought. She'd let Terence slip through her fingers and now found herself stuck with the arrogantly overconfident Steele Hardt. Despite everything, she couldn't deny the simmering-below-the-surface attraction between them. An attraction that could easily compromise any employer-employee relationship.

"Take that yahoo who built the spa, for example. Man, did he give you one hell of a ride." Steele waved the latest missive from the general contractor through the air, then let it fall back onto her desk.

"What exactly makes you some sort of expert? More to the point, how dare you help yourself to private papers in my private office?"

"They were in plain sight. To my mind, the only way a foreman can be any good is if he's privy to what's going on. *Everything* that's going on."

Montana's temper snapped.

"You're fired."

Those wild blue eyes searched her face, as if seeking a sign she was bluffing, before he gave a laconic shrug. "Whatever you say. But first, you owe it to yourself to hear me out."

Chapter Two

"*Do the words 'you're fired'* have no meaning, or have you heard them so often you don't even register the message?"

Steele bit back a smile. He'd never had a real job to speak of, but there was no need to share that piece of information with her.

"I like you, Montana. And I like Black Creek. Things are a bit of a mess right now, but they should be easy enough to put to rights."

"Please leave." When she took hold of his arm as if to physically remove him from her office, his admiration grew. She couldn't budge him, of course, but it was gutsy of her to try.

"I'm really fired, is that right?"

"Correct."

"Good. Because I don't believe in kissing the boss." He pulled Montana into his arms, knowing he had the advantage of surprise on his side, and when she opened her mouth in a soft and startled gasp he covered her lips with his own. She tasted hot and sweet, and after the initial sip he went back for more, deepening the pressure as he pulled her closer.

If ever he'd seen a woman in need of being kissed, it was Montana. He'd heard rumors that her marriage hadn't exactly been a passionate one, which seemed a waste. For simmering just below the surface, he discovered a wellspring of untapped passion. A passion he'd sensed even before they'd met this morning, for only a woman of an intensely passionate nature could appreciate and own a piece by Lamotia.

She started off stiff in his arms. He stroked her back and her shoulders before he slid his hands down over her hips, enjoying the womanly shape of her and the way it juxtaposed his own body. He slanted his mouth against hers for a different angle, a better fit, aware she was starting to soften in his arms, to breathe into him. Encouraged, he continued his gentle exploration. He nibbled her full bottom lip, then pulled it into his mouth before probing its luscious contours. From there he transferred his attention to her Cupid's-bow upper lip, sipping and nibbling as he rubbed his pelvis against her, making her aware of his response.

He felt her jolt of shock at his boldness, but a scant second later she moaned softly in the back of her throat and kissed him back. When he felt her fingers drag through his hair and take hold, he untucked her blouse and helped himself to the warm, supple skin of her back. Her breasts pillowed his chest and he shifted slightly to increase the friction, rewarded by the feel of her nipples hardening against him through the layers of chambray. Her bra wasn't one of those padded numbers, which meant the breasts were as real as the woman herself, and every bit in need of his magic touch as Montana. For in his arms she was all woman, as primed as he was.

The instincts he'd relied on as a world-class gambler and a first-class lover told him Montana was a challenge worth pursuing, a woman worth possessing. A job perk, so to speak.

Damn. Just like that, he'd lost her. His fault for letting his attention wander.

He felt her break the kiss, albeit reluctantly.

"Good thing you fired me," he said huskily, careful to keep one hand against the back of her head, playing with the soft strands of dark brown hair freed from her braid, while his other hand rested on the womanly curve of her waist.

He admired the cameo perfection of her strong yet feminine features. Her skin had a porcelain purity that proclaimed "no sun." She wore no makeup; none was needed to emphasize her striking oval eyes the color of bleached denim, accented by dark brown brows the same color as her thick, straight hair.

She didn't pull away. Instead, she leaned into him, as if unsure whether her legs would support her. He tightened his hold, subliminally telling her he was there for her.

"Right. You'd be an impossible employee."

"I dare you to find out how good I can be."

"Are we talking work? Or other things?"

"You're the boss. You tell me." He kept his voice husky and intimate. When she didn't answer, he continued. "You could reinstate me. Give me a chance to show you what I can do."

She tilted her head to meet his gaze, as if ferreting out his sincerity. Hell, wasn't he the king of sincerity?

"You're used to getting your own way, aren't you?"

"I don't know about that. I know we'd make one hell of a team."

"You don't strike me as a team player, Steele."

"I can be whatever you need me to be. All I'm asking is the chance to prove it." He felt her warming to the idea, warming to him, and mentally congratulated himself as he upped the ante. "Montana, you can't possibly do it all alone. You've got way too much going on for one person."

"Why do you want this so bad?"

"I'm an enlightened guy. I like seeing strong women be successful. Unless you're afraid of me showing you up."

"Afraid? Hardly."

"Then it's settled. I'll look after the ranch so you can concentrate on getting the spa opened on time."

She pursed her lips and he had to curb the urge to kiss her again. "I've got a lot riding on that project."

"Show me."

As he followed her from the ranch house to the brand-new resort and spa, Montana reexamined the fact that she was no longer sure if she what was doing was the right thing.

Was she trying too hard to jam a square peg into a round hole with her plans for Black Creek?

"Sure is pretty country." When Steele stopped in the middle of the footbridge over the creek, Montana stopped as well. The surrounding hills looked black in a certain light, reflecting their color down into the slow-moving waters of the creek, but the ranch name came more from the family than the terrain.

She checked out his profile, hard planes, chiseled angles, and steel-edged jaw. "Where are you from?"

"Pretty much anyplace you can hang a name on."

"I meant originally."

"Well, my mom was a Las Vegas showgirl and my dad was a gambler, and they left my brother and me for my grandfather to raise out in the back of beyond."

He had as nomadic and unsettled a past as she. Even though she had a surfer dad and hippie mom, chasing the next wave from the back of a Volkswagen van, at least she'd been raised by her parents—not stuck away with some old grandparent in the middle of nowhere.

"How was the back of beyond?"

He turned to look at her, and the intimacy, the connection in that look, was unsettling. "Like anything. Whatever you make of it."

"I see." Apparently he didn't care to discuss his past any more than she did hers.

"So, does the spa reflect you and your vision?"

"I'm not sure what you mean."

"What sets Black Creek Spa apart from all the others?

Why would people come here as opposed to, say, someplace in Arizona?"

"You'll have your answer in a minute."

As they talked they'd been walking along the circular driveway from the house to the resort, with its well-maintained grounds. The resort and spa also had a new, separate driveway from the main road and its own parking lot away from the ranch.

Montana unlocked the intricately carved front door of the Oasis and stepped across the threshold, feeling the usual darting thrill chase through her, amplified by the tingling aftereffect of Steele's kiss.

Not only had he caught her off guard, but the swiftness of her own response had startled her. Would she regret keeping him around for a while? Possibly, but for once it didn't seem to matter. Steele was offering to be of use to her in various capacities, and right now she could use all the help she could get.

"Nice," Steele said approvingly as she touched a hidden switch that bathed the reception area in indirect lighting. The whole interior flowed from space to space with curves and rounded edges, no sharp angles or corners to be seen. Black Creek meandered through the lobby ringed by lush greenery, enhanced by subdued lighting.

"I hired the best architecture firm in the country," she said. "I told them to study their most innovative spa design and then do me one better."

A wall of water tumbled softly behind the reception desk, an effective screen to the offices behind.

"I wanted lots of rock and water," Montana explained. "It's important the guests feel they've stumbled across a very private, very decadent underground grotto. All cares should be left behind at the door."

"You'll need to pave the ranch's landing strip," Steele said abruptly.

Montana went rigid. "Whatever for? It's been out of use ever since . . ." Her words trailed off.

"Ever since your husband's accident," Steele finished. "But you'll have guests who will arrive by air. You want to make it as exclusive as possible. I'm thinking along the lines of a special horse and carriage to pick them up and bring them to the resort."

"I never thought of that," Montana said. "It's a great idea."

"All part and parcel of leaving their cares behind, along with day-to-day reality. See where teamwork gets you? Now what's this area over here?"

"That's the beauty parlor. Hair and nails. Treatment rooms are upstairs. But through here is what I'm most excited about."

A softly lit enclosed stairway led the way below to Montana's pièce de résistance.

"It's like entering an underground cave," Steele said.

"Exactly. Welcome to the Hydrawalk," Montana said proudly. "The only one of its kind in North America."

"It's warm down here," Steele said. "I gather it's supposed to be."

"I had it ready to show Terence. When he arrived."

"Good thing I'm here, so it's not wasted."

Montana kept her doubts to herself. "The walk starts over here with these showers. From there you go to the whirlpool, then the waterfalls and steam cave to the . . . What are you doing?"

Steele was stripping off his shirt.

"I've learned that you can talk about a thing, or you can experience it. I go for the experience every time. It's a far better way." As he spoke he sat on a simulated rocky outcropping and pulled off his boots.

"How did you know Charlie died in a plane crash?" She hated the vulnerable catch in her voice. The fact that she hadn't loved Charlie hadn't meant his infidelity hurt any less than his death. At one point she'd considered the tit-for-tat game, having a torrid affair of her own. Maybe if Steele had been here then, she'd have been tempted.

"The way your husband died is common knowledge around these parts. And I believe in knowing who I'm going to be working for."

"Funny. You acted like you didn't know I was a woman when you first arrived."

"I knew, all right. I was just trying to get a rise out of you." Barefoot, he stood and undid the buckle of his belt.

He was getting a rise out of her, all right. The sight of his bare, bronzed chest, ridged with muscle, coupled with the memory of being caught and held against his masculine length was definitely sparking a reaction. An unaccustomed rush of feelings flooded her feminine reaches, like spring thaw after a particularly long winter freeze.

She'd always enjoyed her sexuality, her body and the pleasures it was capable of bringing her, and resented Charlie for his part in the slow death of those feelings. The fact that he'd turned to other women made her feel less of one, less secure in her desirability.

To discover that the sexual side of her wasn't dead, but merely sleeping, was a welcome relief, for she was far too young and vibrant to consider her sex life a thing of the past.

"What are you waiting for?"

She started, then realized he simply meant the Hydrawalk. "Steele, I'm not going skinny-dipping. And neither are you."

"Am I making you uncomfortable?"

"Of course you are. And doing it most deliberately, I'm quite certain." Shirtless, his unbelted jeans barely clinging to his hips, he was the epitome of raw, unsettling masculinity. She recalled his kiss, the light caress of his fingertips across her bare skin and all the inner tingles it ignited. She could chalk up her increased body heat to the temperature in the Hydrawalk, but she knew it was more than that.

"It's good to be uncomfortable. It always leads to new discoveries. What happened to your spa guy?"

"He took a different job. I was counting on him for the final touches and hiring the staff."

"Can't you do that yourself?"

"It looks like I have no other choice. But I believe in delegation."

"So delegate away."

"To you?" She felt as if she were walking a tightrope, with no balance pole and no safety net. What was she thinking bringing Steele here? He unsettled her. He was so damn cocky and arrogant and appealing on all levels.

"Use me and abuse me."

Wouldn't she just love to do that very thing? Montana blew out a breath.

"What's your favorite Hydrawalk station?"

"I haven't tried it out yet. This is the first time it's been ready to go."

"What are you waiting for? Sweetheart, you can't possibly sell something you don't feel passionate about."

"You don't know the first thing about my passions."

"That is where I'd have to call you wrong."

Oh, dear. Montana felt herself drowning in those eyes, awash in the reality of what Steele was saying. For on some subliminal level, he did know her and her passions—fear coupled with exhilaration. He knew what kept her awake at night and what lulled her to sleep. Dreams and ambitions, triumphs and disappointments, he knew them all. Somehow, for whatever it was, for as long as it lasted, she and this man shared a destiny.

Right or wrong, Montana had always made her choices, learned from her mistakes, and moved on. But right now, for the first time ever, things were about to spiral out of her control and she was about to let them.

Montana looked around her grotto, as much a part of her as if she'd given birth to it. Cavernlike walls, tropical plants, and softly falling rain showers all commingled in the steamy moist air and enhanced the otherworldly feel.

She'd conceived the Oasis, nurtured it, and finally

watched it come slowly to life, more amazing and far more wonderful than she had dared to hope.

"This time it's about the letting go. That's why I hired Terence. I feel as if I've done all I can, and now someone else needs to take things to the next level."

He took a self-confident step toward her till they were all but touching. "There's always a next level. And oftentimes it's unnerving to let go of your comfy handgrip in order to reach for it."

"You think I don't know about taking a risk? What do you think this is?" She waved her hands through the air.

"Exactly," he agreed. "And the bigger the gamble, the bigger the payoff, the sweeter the success."

"So long as you don't lose."

"What are you really afraid of losing?"

Herself. Montana snapped her mouth shut before the answer escaped.

Her mother's entire identity had been wrapped up in Montana's father. Montana was the total opposite, distancing herself from others rather than deferring to anyone.

"Montana, look at what you created. You can't possibly lose." He captured her hand in his, slowly linked their fingers, his gaze never leaving hers. "And I'm right here beside you to hold your hand and make sure you don't fall."

She'd never had someone to hold on to, to count on. She didn't know how. She tried to pull back but Steele wouldn't let her.

"Now or never, Montana. Take the plunge."

She slowly reached up and began to unbutton her shirt.

Chapter Three

Steele watched her as if he expected she might change her mind, but due to her upbringing, she had never been prudish. The freedom that came with the way she'd been raised gave her power, along with confidence in her choices.

"You're right," she said, her voice so husky she barely recognized it. "And there's more than one way to take the plunge."

"Eee-yow!"

Montana was still working the buttons of her denim shirt when Steele skinned out of his jeans and cannonballed into the mineral pool with a wild yell.

Montana folded her shirt neatly and set it near the shelves of fluffy new towels by the showers, then slithered out of her jeans, electing to keep on her panties and bra. Not that the lustrous pearl-colored silk thong and matching wisp of a bra provided much coverage, but they added some semblance of modesty.

She was addicted to scrumptious lingerie and the mailman was forever delivering a new package from Victoria's Secret with a wink and a leer; it was an addiction she blamed on her free-spirited mother, who had never owned a bra and certainly never considered buying one for her developing daughter.

Then Montana walked down the carved stone steps and eased into the divinely warm mineral bath with a sigh of pleasure. She leaned back against the simulated rock seat and closed her eyes. She could feel the probe of Steele's striking blue eyes as surely as if he'd reached out and touched her.

"You are in great shape," he said admiringly. "Good genetics or hard work?"

"A little of each," she said, unfazed, as she opened her eyes to skim the planes of his well-defined chest and shoulder muscles. "How about you?"

"Luck and circumstance."

As he spoke he scooted across the pool to stand before her. "I'm a big believer in luck." The water kissed his rib cage as he widened his stance and slowly advanced.

"Good or bad?" she drawled.

"I prefer good."

"I could use a dose of good luck about now, myself."

"Is that a fact?"

She felt the brush of his bare legs against hers in a way that could have been either accidental or deliberate. He was so close, she could see individual droplets of water on the curl of thick, dark eyelashes, and the way dozens of shades of blue colored his irises.

The light spray of a simulated overhead rain shower added to the lush, steamy atmosphere of their own private grotto. Steele raised his head, opened his mouth, and slowly licked his lips, causing a flutter deep within Montana's belly as she recalled the knowing pressure of those shapely lips on hers.

He turned his attention back to her. "Tell me what we're soaking in. It tastes salty."

"This particular pool mimics seawater, with over one hundred essential trace elements and minerals to rebalance and replenish depleted body stores."

"Do you actually buy that?"

"I've seen the scientific data."

"And now you're testing the theory."

"I believe the data."

"And I believe that when you put a naked man and a scantily clad woman in warm water, one thing will inevitably lead to another."

"Are you always so sure of yourself?"

"Always."

Montana laughed. "I have the feeling you might be just what Black Creek needs."

"Not what Montana Blackstone needs?"

"My needs change on an hourly basis."

Steele moved in closer. "My specialty."

"You think you're skilled enough to anticipate and meet my every whim?"

"I'm asking for the chance to try."

"Oh?" She arched an eyebrow. "Then tell me: What do you think I need?"

"You need to be recognized for what you can do. All that you can do."

"True."

"And you need the spa up and running smoothly in time for the grand opening bash you've been busy promoting."

"I do."

"And there are other things that you're not even aware of needing."

"Which would be . . . ?"

"Someone to rub the tension from your shoulders. Someone to listen and share your day-to-day concerns."

"I don't require those things," she said stiffly.

"Not on an ongoing basis, perhaps. But you could use it today. Which is where I come in. You must have a massage table upstairs that could use a test run."

"You list massage among your many and varied talents?"

"I've been told I have a certain flair. Apparently I know some really wicked pressure points."

"Save it, Steele. There are other ways in which you can be of use to me."

"Do tell."

"I'll go one better. I'll show you." As she spoke she rose,

expecting he would yield. She expected wrong. He took full advantage of their close proximity to move in closer, his damp torso flush with her chest. Her sheer silk bra was no barrier and her nipples hardened against the wet silk in a way that was more arousing than if she were wearing nothing at all.

"We haven't renegotiated my contract."

"What did you have in mind?"

"How about a flat fee, renewable on a daily basis? That way if you don't like what I'm doing, we simply walk away from each other, no hard feelings."

"And if I like what you're doing?" she asked with a husky catch in her voice. His nearness stirred something primal inside of her, something she'd feared had been forever extinguished by Charlie's infidelity.

He trailed his fingers down the length of one arm, the light stimulation far more powerful and arousing than if he'd clutched her close. He linked his fingers through hers and raised their joined hands overhead, slowly leaning into her as he pressed her back against the rock. His eyes were on hers with deliberate intent as he pinned her in place.

Montana felt an internal jolt, as if he'd suddenly jump-started something deep within, something that threatened madly to ricochet out of control.

Her breathing quickened. She watched his eyes darken, the pupils dilating till the intriguing rim of blue all but disappeared into the smoldering darkness. He was fully aroused, his body brushing hers with slow and deliberate intent, and she felt herself soften in response, every quivering nerve ending on full alert. She held her breath, wondering what he'd do next. How far would he push her? How intoxicating to yield the control for once.

He kneed her legs apart and pressed his kneecap against that tingling, throbbing central core in a move that both teased and further inflamed her, as he lowered his head and captured her mouth with his own.

Montana shimmied against him, her body suddenly desperately in need of his touch. Everywhere. Fully aroused in a way she'd never been before. His tongue mated with hers, knowing deliberation in the way it challenged and stimulated. He swallowed her soft moan of pleasure, her plea for more as he deepened the kiss and his body molded itself to hers. His erect cock throbbed against the thin barrier of silk as he sought and found her inner heat.

She moaned in frustration, chafed her aching breasts against the crisp matting of damp hair on his chest, and swiveled her pelvis in tandem with his. He broke the kiss, then immediately moved to the sensitive pulse point just below her earlobe, eliciting a low moan for more.

"Turn around," he said, his voice a husky breath of warmth that found its way from her inner ear to her inner womanhood in less than a second.

She did as he said, hands still joined with his as she spun in a graceful arc reminiscent of her short career as a dancer.

He caught both her hands in one of his and anchored them against the rock, imprisoned in a way she found divinely thrilling. His other hand ran freely, knowingly across her breasts, her belly, her hips, and her buttocks, his touch urgent, yet leisurely in his exploration of her body.

How long since she'd been touched by a man? Felt sexy and desired? It was good for her soul, her emotional responses sending her physical reaction right off the Richter scale.

She arched her back and pivoted her hips, feeling the divine hardness of him, so near and yet so far. He responded by pushing her damp hair aside and nibbling the sensitive nape of her neck, his tongue a fiery brand as it snaked the length of her spine.

She thought she might expire with need by the time he slid the thong of her underwear aside and nudged her aching, needy clit with the head of his erection.

She sucked in her breath, closed her eyes, and concentrated on the kaleidoscope of sensations radiating outward from that one central point, as everything else ceased to exist. Her insides wept, more than ready for him.

He applied more pressure as he rubbed and nuzzled once, twice—and on the third pass her world exploded into a myriad of shattered fragments, past and present merging into one fiery ball of ecstatic release.

Fortunately Steele still had hold of her, or she would have sunk beneath the surface as she sagged limply against the rock.

"You've been holding on to that one for a while," he said, his grip firm yet gently possessive, as if he knew she was incapable of standing on her own. He held her close as the aftershocks subsided and the weakness in her limbs slowly passed.

"Better than a handshake to seal our new partnership,"

she said, once she found her voice and turned to face him.

"I'm thinking there must be something to those vitamins and minerals in the water." His cock jutted proudly between them, ramrod straight. She reached for him, closed her fist around his girth, and slowly stroked the length of pulsing male energy. When he responded with a murmur of pleasure she thrilled to the feel of power, the fact that he was equally affected by her touch. She wanted more. She wanted it all.

"Fancy a bit of steam?" she asked.

"Are you implying that I'm not steaming enough for you?"

"Oh, you're hot all right. And about to get even hotter." She led the way to the steam cave, opened the door, and stepped inside. Gauzy swirls of hot steam filled her lungs and obscured vision of all but the closest objects, adding a new dimension to a world where she couldn't see anything except Steele.

"Let's get you out of these wet things," he said. "Sexy as they are."

The admiring look in his eyes brought a fresh rush of desire to her oversensitive nerve endings. She felt as if his eyes were touching her, licking her, admiring her, and she thrilled to the newfound sensations of her female power. She craved his touch, his heat, his possession. She unfastened her bra, shrugged her shoulders, and felt the straps catch on her damp skin. Impatiently he whipped it out of the way. He looked his fill, his eyes so hungry she felt the possessive sizzle of their brand. Then his callused palms paid her breasts homage, tracing their shape and absorbing their texture.

No man had ever touched her with such effect. She felt a pull deep in her womb, a radiant warmth that saturated her limbs. His lightest touch and she was gone. Jelly. Boneless. Aflame for him. Her breasts molded to his palms as if they existed solely for this moment, this man; nipples instantly pouting with neglect when he abandoned them to skim away the tiny triangle guarding her feminine secrets.

"That's better," he murmured. "Skin on skin."

"Yes." She touched him as he touched her, helping herself to the bulging curve of his biceps before following the tangle of chest hair that fanned his flat abdomen, ringed his navel, and nested his cock and his balls.

She licked her palm to moisten it, then closed her fist around him. Slowly she ran her fisted hand from tip to root of his impressive length. He was hot to the touch, pulsing, and she licked her lips in anticipation of his possession. Unleashing the full force of his power.

"So soft and yet so hard," she murmured. His skin was soft, his muscled frame hard, yielding to her touch and fitting perfectly against hers.

He picked her up effortlessly and set her on the smoothly curving bench seat of the cave. He knelt before her, gently stroking her knees and thighs till her muscles relaxed and grew slack. She felt herself opening for him inside and out, as his smoldering gaze discovered each and every one of her secrets. Steam surrounded her, saturated her, poured through her as, beneath the intensity of his admiring look, he coaxed her legs apart to sample her delicate inner womanhood.

A rush of sensation threatened to overtake her as his

knowing lips and tongue first outlined the outer petals of her lower lips, then found their way to the engorged and throbbing inner pearl of her clitoris.

Back and forth his head moved, teasing, tasting, nibbling, from inner thigh to inner lips, finally reaching the prize. His attention, so light and teasing, barely more than a breath, aroused her beyond all sanity, yet it denied her body's clamor for relief as the roiling pressure continued to build inside her.

Her breathing grew harsh, taking on the desperate focus of a sprinter approaching the finish line.

"Wait for me." He stood, then seated himself with her straddling his lap.

With a sob of relief she fisted her hands behind his neck and lowered herself slowly onto him. She groaned in ecstasy at the slick feel of him filling her, stretching her, their bodies a perfect fit.

She shuddered as her orgasm ripped through her, felt him tense and fight for control as she rocked back and forth, her control shattered by the eruptions exploding deep within. She sagged against him, the slickness of their skin a further arousal, and took a second to catch her breath.

He tilted her head up and kissed her, his tongue invading her mouth with a devouring hunger that fed the force of their joining. She repositioned her legs so that she was kneeling, able to achieve more friction as she climbed aboard for round two.

"More," she breathed.

He moved accommodatingly.

"Greedy," he said.

"Starving," she corrected.

They moved together, his hands on her hips setting the pace at which she rode him, bucking and rearing as his slick, hot cock slid in and out—first fast, then slow, then fast again till, with a muffled groan, he lifted her off of him. His hard cock slid up and down the soft, responsive lips of her labia, grazing her hungry opening, the head kissing her clit.

With a triumphant cry of surrender he clenched and shuddered, and a milky spray of semen shot between them. He pulled her tight to him, their perspiration mingling with the spill of his release. "I didn't have a condom," he said by way of explanation, and she was touched by his thoughtfulness.

"Nothing wrong with an enriched vitamin and mineral spa treatment."

Chapter Four

They'd showered in silence, fancy-schmancy showers with half a dozen showerheads coming at them from all directions, before they dressed and left the hushed confines of the grotto. Upstairs, Steele whistled tunelessly as he watched Montana flick switches and reset timers, shutting down the Hydrawalk, all the while avoiding any eye contact.

Did she really intend to act as if nothing had happened? he wondered. It was only sex, a healthy workout—not much different from a well-matched game of tennis.

Once she seemed satisfied all was in order, they walked through the dusky start of nightfall to the ranch house.

When it still didn't seem she was going to speak up, Steele broke the silence.

"I know you can do what has to be done on your own, but it'll be easier with my help," he said. "If you're still of that mind." Never let it be said he didn't know when to hold 'em and when to fold 'em. He was offering her the chance to bow out gracefully if that's what she wanted.

"I'll accept your offer."

"Excellent. We'll reconvene in the morning." He left her at the front door and went to the bunkhouse, where a game of Texas Hold 'em was under way.

"Care to sit in, Steele?" Zeb spoke around a toothpick lodged in the corner of his mouth as he shuffled the well-worn deck of casino cast-offs.

"Rain check." Steele ignored the snigger and barely audible slur on his sexual preferences. He'd met the ranch hands earlier that day and could already predict who would resent his presence.

Don, the youngest of the group, was winning big, and it took Steele only a minute to figure he had a couple of aces squirreled away. Steele couldn't abide cheaters, the worst kind of loser possible.

Since the men were focused on their hole cards, no one noticed when Steele palmed the aces from an identical deck over near the crib board. Nice thing about the casino cast-offs, they were all the same.

He sauntered over to the stove, poured himself a mug of powerful-looking coffee, and waited for the right moment to make his move. For what was poker if not a waiting game? A few more hands were played, and Don continued to clean up amid good-natured grumbles. Apparently it wasn't the first time Don had been "lucky." Time to get in there before the others gave up and called it a night.

"Maybe I'll sit in a few, after all." Steele bought his chips and eased into the game, paying more attention to the other men than his own cards. He played easy, folded after the flop, and soon it was his turn to deal. The deck was swollen from overuse and noticeably light; Don definitely had two aces. Steele deliberately fumbled the cards so that several landed face up.

Don made a loud sound of disgust, but he was greedy. He'd stick around a while longer.

"Sorry," Steele said to no one in particular as he swept the cards across the tabletop. "These needed a wash anyway." He put the deck back together, knowing Don had both black aces.

Once everyone had their hole cards and made their bets, he dealt the flop and slid the missing black aces into position.

Don was getting excited, his color as high as his overconfident bet. When Steele flipped over the river, the ace of spades he knew Don was planning to play, the other man's deflation was classic. He gave Steele a hard look, then threw in his cards in disgust while the others finished up the round. Steele folded as well. "Having bad luck with the aces, my friend?"

"Not till now."

"Shame." As the next dealer started to shuffle the cards, Steele reached for his stacks of chips. The others watched open-mouthed as he shuffled the stacks, mixing up the colors and then re-separating them to solid-color columns, smooth as silk.

He pushed back his chair. "Thanks for letting me sit in, boys. It's been a while."

A burly older cowboy named Reggie spoke up. "I knew you looked familiar. I've seen you in the tournaments. Till you up and quit one day."

"Retired," Steele said smoothly. "Thought it was time I got back to my roots. There's something more real about working the land."

"You miss it?" asked the redhead named Thomas.

"Nah," Steele said. "How could I possibly miss the tables when I have the chance to work with you pros?"

The men laughed and got up. A few slapped him on the back, and Steele expected he'd have no resistance from them with any changes he planned.

Montana would be a whole other matter.

An hour later, he received an emergency call from Sloan that made him hightail it out of there for the ranch up north where he and his brother had grown up. By the time he arrived, in the middle of the night, breaking every speed limit he encountered, his grandfather's condition had stabilized.

"Sorry for the false alarm, bro," Sloan said once Steele had seen for himself that the man who raised them was resting easy. "Dragged you up here for nothing."

"No problem. I'd kill you if the old man took a bad turn and no one let me know."

"He's supposed to watch his diet and lay off the booze, but you know him; stubborn as they come. And I can't watch him every minute of the day."

"No one expects you to," Steele said. "He'll make his own choices, same as he taught us."

"God willing, he'll outlive us all," Sloan said as he poured two glasses of eighteen-year-old Glenfiddich, then passed one to Steele. "You leaving right away?"

"I've got something I need to get back to."

"Something, or someone?" Sloan asked.

"A bit of both," Steele said, with a knowing wink. "How's your romantic life?"

Sloan shrugged. "You got the glamour gig while I got to keep the home fires burning here."

"Ours was always a partnership. I made the money, the rest of you spent it."

"Invested it, you mean," Sloan scoffed. "And now you're set. You never wore out that golden touch you're so famous for."

Steele clinked his glass with Sloan's. "They don't call me Midas for nothing."

By the time he and Sloan finished chewing the fat about the old days, he only had a few hours to sleep before he made the long return journey to Black Creek.

He found Montana in the spa unloading inventory, not at all pleased to see him.

He ignored her cold shoulder and studied the rows of double-padded lounge chairs, like those you'd see on a cruise ship or alongside a pool.

"What's this place?"

"It's called the relaxation room."

"How come you're not relaxing?"

"Unlike you, I have things to do." She straightened and pushed a loose strand of hair out of her face. "I thought you had up and run off."

"Didn't you get my message?"

"What message?"

"I had a family emergency. I told Zeb to make sure you knew I'd be back later today."

She crossed the room and turned her back on him, fiddling with a box of stuff. "Zeb never said a word."

Interesting. "I guess he must have misunderstood. Anyway, I'm back. You needn't be so happy to see me."

"Don't flatter yourself," Montana said. "It wouldn't have surprised me a bit if you'd left for good. After all, you came, you saw, and you conquered."

Steele realized she was worried about how the sex might change things between them, but she was throwing up her barriers far too late. As a professional card player, he'd learned early on never to expose either your strength or your weakness. It was a lesson Montana would benefit from, but he wasn't the one to teach her.

"I'll talk to Zeb," Steele said.

"Black Creek is my ranch. My problem."

"I thought you hired me to lift a few of those weights off of your pretty shoulders."

"Here. Lift this, tough guy!" She thrust a heavy carton into his arms so abruptly, he nearly dropped it.

"What is it, bricks?"

"It's mud from the Dead Sea. Rich in minerals and antioxidants."

"You're big on minerals around here, aren't you?"

"Why don't you go take care of the ranch, Steele, and let me take care of the spa?"

"I thought we had a partnership."

"Wrong. What we had was a very intense and invigorating sexual escapade yesterday. One I enjoyed very much. But that's not why you're here."

"Women aren't the only ones who can multitask," he said. "Where does this mud go?"

"Into the supply closet at the end of the hall, past the treatment rooms."

He couldn't resist a peek inside the box. Yup, it was mud, all right.

"What kind of treatment do the guests get with this goop?"

"First it's heated in the microwave, so it's soft and warm before being spread all over the client, who is then wrapped in plastic so the properties are absorbed into the skin."

"Are you telling me the client is naked? And some lucky bastard gets to rub mud all over them?" He tried to coax a smile from her. "How do I get into that line of work?"

She shot him an exasperated look. "Seems to me you make out just fine. Don't you have a fence to go mend, or something?"

He shifted the box of mud to his other arm. "Are you going to tell me what's really bugging you, or just make me guess?"

"No more games, Steele. I've got work to do."

"We both have work to do, and it strikes me we'll be a lot more effective doing it together."

"I disagree." She faced him, arms folded across her chest in a pose that screamed defensive. He'd honed his reputation watching other people, reading their body language. "Don't forget I fired you once. I can easily do it again."

He gave no response, letting the silence speak for itself as her words trailed into nothingness.

"Ever need someone, Montana? Really need someone to the point that you couldn't imagine your life without them?"

"I don't know what you mean."

"I mean that you're afraid. Afraid to actually need someone, and to admit it out loud."

She forced a laugh. "I suppose you're arrogant enough to think I need you."

"I wasn't referring to myself. I'm talking about the universal physical human need that's buried deeper in some of us than in others. Some hide it so deep, even the thought of it becomes their greatest fear."

"Don't try to psychoanalyze me, Steele." She reached to tear the box of mud from his arms, and when he hung on she pulled harder. Abruptly he let go.

She wasn't expecting his capitulation and the sudden lack of resistance sent her flying backward to land three feet away, the upended box of mud oozing all over her.

Steele tried not to laugh and thought he managed quite well, with only an earsplitting grin showing his amusement as he stepped forward and held out his hand to help her up.

She let him pull her upright, then hurled herself at him in a full-on tackle that left him equally mud-coated.

He regained his balance, dove for the box of mud, and scooped out a handful.

"Oh, no you don't!" She saw him coming, his intention clear. He mushed the mud between his palms and advanced slowly and steadily, backing her into a corner. When her eyes darted from side to side, he knew she was planning to dart past him. He feinted first to the left, then to the right, but she was fast. She had just gotten by him when the door opened behind him and sent him flying into her, knocking them both off balance.

When he reached to steady her, she raised her hands to fend him off, with the result that they both wound up wearing more mud.

"I hope I'm not interrupting." Helen's eyes were bright as her gaze traveled from one to the other, and she handed Montana the cordless phone. "I thought this call might be important. It's long distance."

"Thanks." Still watching Steele from the corner of her eye, she wiped her muddy hands on the hem of his shirt and took the phone. Helen closed the door as she left.

"Black Creek Resort and Spa. Montana Blackstone speaking."

Steele watched in admiration as she switched on her professional voice. The person on the other end of the phone would have no clue that she was a step away from mud wrestling.

"Sure. Let me put you on hold for a sec while I have my secretary check my calendar." He watched her press the hold button, stare at the ceiling, and count to twelve under her breath before she resumed the conversation.

"Good news," she said sweetly. "I can fit you in that day . . . Shall we say ten a.m. here at the spa? . . . Excellent, I look forward to it."

She ended the conversation and thrust the phone in the air in victory.

"Good news?"

"An interview with *Spa* magazine," she said. "They got wind of the Hydrawalk." She set down the phone on the counter and turned on the tap at the sink.

"What are you doing?"

"Washing up, of course. What do you think?"

He came up behind her. The mirror over the sink framed their image as he pushed aside the collar of her shirt and nibbled the sweet spot where shoulder curved into neck.

"I think it's a sin to waste all those minerals." As he spoke, he unbuttoned her shirt and unhooked her bra in one slick move. She shuddered as he slowly, deliberately smoothed mud across her breasts, kneading her nipples into hard little pleasure points.

"Steele, you're making a mess."

But her breath caught and nothing in her tone or her body's sway toward him suggested he ought to stop what he was doing. Quite the contrary. She was leaning into him, so hot the mud melted beneath his hands and spread across her skin like sun-warmed chocolate as he peeled away her shirt and his. He slicked more mud across her back, then rubbed against her with his chest. He felt her shudder, encouraging him to do more. He slid his hands down the back of her jeans and cupped the round curves of her ass, giving a gentle squeeze.

She turned in his arms to face him, caught his face in her hands, and pulled him down for her kiss. A needy, hungry kiss that drank from him the way parched soil gobbles up droplets of rain. Her tongue swept through the cavern of his mouth while her lips sipped and nipped and murmured, little sighing sounds of pleasure and want that echoed through his bloodstream and headed straight for his eager-to-please joy-stick.

When he unfastened her jeans and peeled them from her hips, she swayed from side to side in an effort to help; at the same time her hands went to his waistband and fumbled with the fastening.

He didn't realize she had a handful of mud until the cold dampness hit. Talk about shrinkage! But not for long, the way Montana slid her mud-slick fist up and down his cock.

He helped himself to a handful and spread it on her mons, feeling her heat radiate and soften the mud, making it as spreadable as warm honey.

"Is it edible?" he murmured against her lips, his finger finding the pulsing nubbin of her clit.

"'Fraid not," she murmured, moving against his finger, encouraging him to continue with his attentions. He felt her muscles tense, felt a ripple of response as her body's moist excitement made the mud a potent lubricant.

She ran her hands over his back and his ass, the slickness of the mud in delightful contrast with the rasp of her nails.

"That's a shame," he said. "But you'll be happy to know I brought a condom this time."

"Only one?"

Chapter Five

"How many do you think I'm going to need?" He felt the concentrated way she rode his hand and knew a sudden surge of pleasure at the anticipation of her riding him with the same enthusiasm.

"That all depends on your rate of recovery." Her breath speeded up, lids half closed, eyes glazed with desire while her fingers dug into his shoulders, clutching him as if her life depended on it.

"With you? Seconds."

"That's good. Because I need you."

"Need me how?"

"I need you hard. I need you in me."

"Do you want me to stop this?" He slowed the speed with which he stimulated her and her thighs clenched his hand, her opening hot and hungry.

"Don't . . . you . . . dare! Ahhhhh!"

She flung her head back as a shudder radiated through her from top to toe, like a dam bursting open. Gradually her limbs grew slack, her hold on him relaxing, and he slid his hand from between her legs, replacing it with the tip of his ramrod-stiff cock.

Who was he teasing more? Her or himself? His sensitive glans absorbed the gentle ripplelike aftershocks as he rubbed and rooted. Her clit still pulsed faintly and he found the sensation far more arousing than if she'd boldly reached for him. Her internal heat poured over him, through him, surrounded him till he felt he'd explode if he didn't bury himself fully inside her.

He propelled her to the nearest lounger and stopped to grab a condom from his jeans. She opened her arms to him, opened herself to him, and he was gone. He'd wanted to take it slow, to tease her to several more pleasure peaks, but when she wrapped those long legs of hers around his middle and all but inhaled him, all thoughts vanished save the most primitive urge to drive himself into her.

She loved it. Bucking and writhing beneath him, she met thrust for thrust, taking as good as she got. Her nails dug into his back, his ass.

"Faster. Harder. *More.*"

"I'll give you more." She was a wild woman beneath him,

scissoring her legs for more friction, deeper penetration, so sweet, so hot and tight, that he was afraid he'd come too soon. He pulled out reluctantly, despite her efforts to keep him there and her murmur of complaint. He rubbed her clit with the head of his cock, circled it, teased her by almost going in, then pulling back to caress that most responsive part of her again.

He felt it at the same time she did. A shudder that seemed to start in her toes and ripple up her legs like the swell of a tsunami, powering through her in a rush. Whew! He waited for the waves to recede before he allowed himself back in.

Slower this time, he absorbed her calm, then steadily pumped to rebuild her peak. It didn't take long before she was panting and moaning beneath him again, her body strung tense and tight once more, her hands frantic on him.

He paused and looked her straight in the eye to let her know he was there and not about to disappoint her. He kissed her, absorbed her frenzy, tempered it, then let it swell in tandem with his.

As she bucked from side to side beneath him he finally let himself go, caught in the maelstrom of her passionate release. Together they crested wave after wave of orgasmic bliss that rolled through her into him, finally taking him with her to the ultimate pinnacle of ecstasy.

"Wow!" He lay heavily atop her, totally limp. He thought he ought to move, but she didn't seem to mind.

"Wow, yourself." She wrapped her arms around him. Her internal muscles pulsed, bathing him in the backwash, and he couldn't have moved if he tried.

She toyed with his hair where it brushed his ear. "I hope you weren't bragging about your powers of recovery."

He laughed. "I hope I wasn't, too." But hell, he was only human, he needed a breather. "How'd you wind up being called Montana?"

"My mother said that's where I was conceived. I didn't believe her, though—there're no waves there."

He must have looked blank, because she added, "My dad was a surfer. He followed the waves up and down the coast, from the Baja to the Pacific Northwest and into Canada."

"What about you and your mother?"

"We went with him."

"All year round?"

"Yup. Home was a Volkswagen van. Dad surfed and Mom made macramé and jewelry to sell at craft markets. Sometimes we'd get a few days' work at a farm picking fruit or vegetables. Then we'd be off."

"No school? No home? No friends?" He couldn't imagine such a lifestyle. His own had been unorthodox enough, but at least he'd had a solid roof over his head, and solid earth under his feet.

"We made friends on the road. My mom and some of the others home-schooled whatever kids were around. Everyone looked out for everyone else."

"Not much privacy in a van," Steele mused.

"None," Montana said matter-of-factly. "Sex was never hidden or something to be ashamed of. Just part of life."

She was silent for a long minute. "My dad died when I was twelve. Melanoma got a lot of those surfer guys."

"Then what happened?" He stroked her shoulder, encouraging her to go on. He doubted Montana was in the habit of opening up, any more than he was.

"We stopped moving around. My mom got remarried. I had to go to a real school, where they skipped me with kids years older. I never fit in. Not just because of my age, but everything. I didn't shop and talk on the phone and gossip. It all seemed so stupid. So I finished school fast and struck out on my own. Eventually I went to college; later I met and married Charlie."

There were big gaps in the story, but he had a few secrets of his own. She was entitled.

"How long were you married?"

"It would have been ten years."

"Ever wish you could just chuck it all and go back on the road, like when you were a kid?"

She gave him an incredulous look. "Why would I want to do that?"

"Sometimes the good old days just seem so good."

"Today is tomorrow's good old day."

"So it is." He rolled to his side, tugging her with him. "Do you think we've absorbed enough minerals from this mud that it's actually done us some good?"

"Absolutely."

"Then I vote for a shower."

"Good idea."

The room she led him into was completely tiled, floor and walls, with drain holes in the floor and a lounge in the middle. The ceiling light was muted, more of an ethereal glow.

"Lie there on your stomach," she said, indicating the lounge. "I'll join you in a second."

While he lay there she swung a long metal rod out from the wall, positioned high over the bed. The room fogged with steam as warm water pulsed from dozens of shower-heads in the rod and massaged every part of his body. Montana joined him, like a mermaid from the mist, and he was pleased to note his powers of recovery hadn't let him down. He closed his eyes and simply enjoyed the sensations of warm, pulsating water and warm, pulsating woman. Montana sleeked atop him, her arms around his neck, her damp hair teasing the back of it. He could feel her groin snug against his ass, her legs clasping his. Her breasts were flattened against his back, but not for long—for as the shower continued its magic massage, so did Montana.

She knelt just over him and he could feel the teasing brush of her breasts, the faint prickle of her closely trimmed pubic hair. She moved across him like an exotic dancer, teasing, brushing, warm, wet skin, all hot and aroused.

He rolled over. He wanted to see her. And she was magnificent. Strong, supple limbs, writhing and maneuvering; now she touched him, now she didn't. She used every part of her body, played with him as if she were a cat and he the powerless mouse, mesmerized by her power. Totally defenseless.

It was a new pose for him.

Her fingertips drummed across his chest, lighter than the water droplets, more elusive, as she shimmied down his length.

When she took his cock into her mouth, her fall of water-darkened hair like a curtain between them, he stifled a groan of pleasure.

Then she swept her hair aside so he could see her lips moving up and down his shaft, the way her tongue darted in and out with teasing strokes.

She licked him as if he were melting ice cream and she was determined not to miss a drop. He heard her murmur of pleasure as she ran her tongue along the underside, paused to delicately flick his balls, then move on from root to head. She sucked him gently, as if he were fragile as an egg, her mouth exerting the barest of pressure. Torture most exquisite.

"God, Montana." He enjoyed it till he could bear no more. "Come up here," he said. "I want to love your breasts."

Sinewy as a cat, she slid up him, fulfilling his every wish. Her breasts, plump and soft and round, dangled just above him like the ripest, most delicious fruit. She swayed slightly, dragging them side to side across his face and through his greedy, open mouth.

He caught them together in his hands, opened wide, and devoured them.

She made little mewling noises of pleasure. Was a woman ever more designed for loving? Just the way she moved, her heat, her response—he had to have her *all.*

He repositioned her till she knelt directly above him, her beautiful pink pussy delectably within reach. He buried his face in her softness and gorged himself on her amazing taste.

As he felt her initial wave of response, he held her hips. He'd never had a woman come this way before. She sobbed softly at first, panting breaths that drove him crazy, as he determined to drive her higher. Then she reared up and screamed in pleasure, a primally wild sound that echoed through the tile room, almost enough to get him off as well.

When she rolled off of him and reached for his cock he pulled away, ready to explode.

"Come here."

He was amused by her bossiness, her take-charge attitude, and infinitely curious to see what she had in mind next.

Once he was kneeling above her, she shifted beneath him till he straddled her breasts. She pushed them together, gloving his cock in their soft warmth.

He ached, hard and hot, and her breasts seemed to melt around him as he plunged in and out of the tight crevice she designed. He thumbed her nipples with one hand as he reached behind and found her central core. He barely touched her clit before he felt her undulation of pleasure. He bit his lower lip, trying to exercise the steel control on which he prided himself, but it was futile. The sight of his hard cock plunging in and out of the pale chasm of her breasts while her entire body pulsed with delight was his undoing. Steele collapsed atop her, totally spent, while the warm shower caressed him with its soothing massage.

He'd barely settled into place when Montana wriggled out from beneath him, gave a satisfied stretch, then rose to turn off the water.

"How can you move?"

"Sex invigorates me." She tossed him an oversized towel and wrapped herself in its mate.

"Lucky you." He ignored the towel; he felt like he could just sleep forever.

She was magnificent! He had no doubt she'd succeed at whatever she set her mind to. Unfortunately that wasn't the type of thing that needed to be in his final report. Facts and figures were required. Information he needed to either charm out of Montana or come up with on his own.

He watched her dry off and run the towel through her hair.

"Clean up this mess, would you? It looks like someone had a mud fight upstairs."

"Sorry, doll." He rolled off the bed. Every nerve ending thrummed with soul-deep sexual satisfaction. "That's not why I was hired."

"I hope we're not going to go through this any time I tell you to do something."

"I hope not, too." He advanced toward her, purpose in his stride.

"Maybe we could clean up together. Like the team we profess to be."

"We make a damn good team, in and out of bed."

She got quiet at that. "Teammates need to trust each other."

"Don't you trust me, Montana?" She couldn't have any idea why he was really here, or who arranged it, could she?

She shook her head as she shrugged into a white terry robe. "Not for a second."

"Hmph." He digested that one. Usually he could bluff

and charm his way into anyone's favors. What made Montana different?

Likely the same thing that made this entire job different. Montana was harder to read than most. Maybe that was it. He'd gotten used to playing with the pros and they were consistent. Montana was neither a pro nor consistent. Which meant he had to change his tactics.

"You go on ahead. I'll take care of things here," he said.

"You will?" She wasn't kidding that she didn't trust him.

"Sure. I know how to use a mop and a washing machine."

"Excellent."

He watched her leave as if she couldn't get away fast enough. This teamwork thing was starting to feel like a bad idea. He was used to assessing the situation and calling the shots himself, delegating where feasible but mostly doing things on his own. How was this going to work out?

Montana burst outside for air; sparring with Steele always left her feeling breathless.

"Montana, a word, please."

Drat, it was Bradley, the ranch cook. And she in a terry robe.

"What is it, Bradley?" He was a big man, and looked even bigger in his kitchen whites.

"Some hoity-toity catering company called, asking about the kitchen facilities for the grand opening party. Why don't you want *me* to make the food for it?"

"Bradley, you have enough to do as it is, feeding everyone on the ranch. I can't expect you to handle the party, as well."

"My chili is a prizewinner every year," Bradley said, with the beginning of a pout.

"And it's fabulous," Montana said. "But this is for the spa and the resort, not the dude ranch."

"Food that looks pretty with no taste," Bradley said disparagingly. "What's wrong with good old-fashioned stick-to-the-ribs food? I've been cooking it like that forever."

"And the ranch guests all love your cooking," Montana said. "But the resort guests will have different expectations."

"Is that why you didn't consult with me on the new kitchen?"

She hadn't realized he was feeling hurt and left out.

"Bradley, I'm sorry that I didn't make things clear. You won't be working in the new kitchen. I'm going to hire another chef for the spa."

"Do I need to look for a new job?"

"Heavens, don't you dare! What would I do without you?"

Somewhat mollified, he lumbered back to his kitchen.

Thankfully, she was dressed before her next interruption.

"Montana, dear."

Montana inwardly cringed. She knew that tone meant Helen was up to something.

"I hope it's all right with you; I've invited Steele and Zeb up to the house tonight for dinner."

"Why would you do that?"

"Well, I think Zeb's nose is a little out of joint that you brought Steele in."

"*You* brought Steele in," Montana reminded her.

"And you have to agree, it was a good idea."

"Not if there's a mutiny with the ranch hands," Montana retorted.

"It's only Zeb, dear. He needs to feel that he's more than just another member of the staff."

"So they need to bond, is that it?"

"Zeb's been here so long, I suspect he's just a little resistant to all the changes. That's all."

"He knows there will always be a place here for him."

"Good! Then dinner's at seven," Helen said. "And Montana, make an effort to get out of those dreadful jeans for a change."

Montana shot her a suspicious look. "What are you up to, Helen?"

"Not a thing. I just think it's good for a woman to dress the part once in a while."

The door closed behind her, and Montana went back to culling through the résumés that had been flooding in since she'd advertised for spa staff. If Terence hadn't let her down, he'd be doing this and she could concentrate on other things. Steele had offered to help her, but she'd refused. His responsibilities started and stopped on the ranch. True, he needed to look at the big picture, but if she didn't draw a line in the sand and stick to it, he'd stomp all over her boundaries.

Chapter Six

When Montana arrived for dinner she saw Zeb standing off to one side, barely recognizable without his chaps and his Stetson, and Helen, overdressed in brocade pants and matching top, sitting practically on top of Steele. Diamonds winked at her throat and ears as she touched him frequently while relating some story.

"Drink, Montana?" Helen asked brightly.

"I'll get it." Montana headed for the martini pitcher. "You look extremely comfortable." As did Steele.

Helen patted Steele's thigh. "Steele is full of wonderful stories."

Steele looked up at Montana and winked. "Just so you remember, Helen, that's all they are: stories."

"This was a great idea," Montana said as she joined the trio. If she had to see Steele, it was better in a group.

Helen preened. "I had such fun, menu-planning with the cook. Montana and I do get in a rut with our evening meals."

Montana felt a twinge of guilt. Charlie had completely spoiled Helen while he was alive, and lately Montana had let things slide. She'd gotten into the habit of working late and eating alone later—no more formal dinners like the three of them had always had.

Montana caught the unhappy look that crossed Zeb's face. "How's your beer, Zeb?"

He scowled at the import bottle in his hand. "Don't know why we got to drink this European stuff when the U.S. of A. makes a perfectly good brew."

Montana saw Helen's quick look of hurt. "At least she didn't make you have it in a glass."

"Good thing," Zeb muttered, smoothing his slicked-back hair as if self-conscious.

"You look nice all gussied up," Montana told him.

"It isn't every night I get invited to dinner at the big house."

"That's my fault," she said in an attempt to dispel the growing tension. "I've been so busy with the resort, I haven't made much time for socializing."

"How long till the grand opening?" Helen asked.

"Less than two weeks. I'm counting on you to rope in a posse of your society friends."

"Don't you worry. Everyone loves a party."

"I hope so." She couldn't allow herself to consider failure; Black Creek was all she had. If it failed, she failed.

"Have you hired the resort staff yet?"

She ground her teeth at Steele's innocent tone. "Things are under control." She had told the exact same lie to Melvin, the resort's main backer, the last time he checked in. Come to think of it, Melvin had been suspiciously silent lately. He must have figured she had enough on her plate without him pestering her, as well.

She raised her glass in a toast. "To the success of Black Creek's new enterprise."

"May it be the first of many," Steele said.

"Indeed," echoed Helen.

All eyes turned to Zeb, who was noticeably silent.

"Y'all said it for me," he said, taking a pull of his beer. Montana noticed his eyes never left Helen.

Montana concentrated on her martini. It was bone dry and icy cold. "You haven't lost your touch," she told Helen. "Perhaps I should hire you to tend bar in the resort."

She'd meant it as a joke, knowing Helen had never had anything resembling a job in her life. But the quick flush of interest lighting up Helen's features told her to pay attention.

"Shall we adjourn to the dining room?" Helen rose and Zeb rushed to her side and offered her his arm.

"Allow me."

Helen giggled like a schoolgirl. "Why, Zeb. You never fail to amaze me."

"You haven't seen anything yet."

Steele rose leisurely and made his way to Montana's side. "I can't have the old boy showing me up now, can I?" He ran his hand across her back, brushing her shoulder blades in an intimate way. Fortunately Zeb and Helen were totally absorbed in each other and didn't witness his blatant familiarity. If this was what happened when you slept with the help—they started taking liberties in public—no wonder they had to be fired afterward.

Once everyone was seated, Montana determined to keep the conversation more business oriented. "Any concerns on the ranch side of things?" she asked Zeb.

"Best I've seen," Zeb said. "Boys are happy. Guests are happy."

"No more problems with Don?"

"Steele put him right in his place first day out," Zeb said admiringly. "You should have seen him in action."

"Really?" Montana said, her interest piqued. "How so?"

"Nothing, really," Steele said, looking uncomfortable for once. "Just a little sleight of hand I picked up in Vegas."

"You should have seen those chips fly. I'll tell you, he got the instant respect of all the hands."

"Really," Montana said. "Perhaps you'll give us a little demonstration after we eat."

"It's nothing you ladies would find of interest."

"On the contrary, I'm always interested in anything that earns the instant respect of my ranch hands."

After a decidedly awkward silence, Helen spoke up. "You'll tell me what I can do to help with the grand opening, won't you, Montana?"

Montana knew that it was important Helen feel part of the changes at Black Creek, for it had been her home long before Montana arrived on the scene.

"I think the biggest help you could be is to run interference between the resort kitchen and the ranch kitchen. Bradley's feeling were hurt that he's not doing the food."

"I'll take care of Bradley for you," Helen said, with a coy smile.

Montana hoped Helen didn't mean things the way they sounded, and judging from Zeb's sudden scowl, she wasn't the only one with that concern.

She continued, "It's important that everyone who's been part of Black Creek for a long time realizes these changes are for the best. Once I have the resort and spa staffed, I plan to offer longtime workers complimentary spa services so they can see what it's all about."

Zeb let out a snort, echoed by Steele's amused chortle.

"What's so funny?" Montana looked from one to the other.

"You're not getting these old cowpokes in to get their nails buffed, Montana," Zeb scoffed.

Montana looked to Helen for support. "We're planning special spa packages just for men."

"Zeb's right, Montana. I know you mean well, but some of these guys are the last dinosaurs to roam the earth. They wouldn't be caught dead going to a spa."

"Fine. Then let's hear your ideas so I don't alienate my longtime workers."

"Zeb and I'll chew this one over and get back to you."

As the others chitchatted through the remainder of the meal, Montana's brain was in full overdrive. Why did she suddenly feel that if she wasn't careful, she was about to lose total control of her dream?

She studied Steele across the table. As if on cue, he looked up and held her gaze, while at the opposite end of the table Zeb and Helen were chatting away. Clearly Helen had smoothed things over with Zeb.

Helen was just suggesting after-dinner cognac back in the sitting room when Steele unclipped his cell phone from his belt and frowned at the caller ID screen. "Please excuse me for a moment."

He went over for a low-voiced exchange with Zeb, who started to rise, but Steele's arm on the older man's shoulder stilled the movement.

"There's no reason for both of us to rush over there," Steele said.

"A smart man doesn't go alone."

"What's the problem?" Montana asked.

"I need to see to something with one of the ranch guests."

"I'll go with you," Montana said.

"That's not necessary," Steele said.

"But smart," Zeb said.

"Teamwork," Montana reminded him.

"Suit yourself." Steele gave in with poor grace.

Helen stared at the doorway in the wake of Montana and Steele's exit.

"Ever wonder if you've done the right thing, Zeb?"

"Folks mostly end up regretting things they don't do; best just try to learn from the rest."

"That's a very interesting observation."

"You hired the boy. That what's got you wondering?"

"I suppose."

"Montana likely figured you hired him 'cause you fancy him."

"And she can keep right on thinking that. Do you have past regrets, Zeb?"

"One pretty big one. Something I should have done years ago and never did."

She leaned forward, intrigued. "They say it's never too late."

Zeb cleared his throat noisily and took a swallow of his cognac. "Do you believe that?"

"That it's never too late? I'd like to think so. What is it you regret not doing?"

"This." Zeb leaned forward and kissed Helen full on the mouth.

Out front, Montana climbed into the waiting golf cart next to Steele. The moon was nearly full, lightly swathed in wisps of cloud, a beacon in a magical patchwork sky of stars. Breathing deeply of night air spiced with the sweet scent of jasmine, Montana realized she'd been so focused on the resort that she hadn't taken the time lately to appreciate her surroundings. Black Creek had always been a special place.

"Which cabin did the call come from?"

"Spur. The guest claims there's something wrong with her shower."

Montana fell silent. There had been a time past when she knew the names and cabins of all Black Creek guests, particularly the regulars. Was she doing the right thing, trying to expand without destroying the integrity of the ranch?

"Don't tell me you're a plumber, along with your other varied talents."

"Just trying to be a good foreman."

"Isn't Lilith working Guest Services?"

"That's who called me." He stopped the cart in front of Spur, its faded wood siding gilded silver in the moonlight. The cabin's front door was ajar, spilling a wedge of light across the wooden porch. Steele rapped loudly on the open door. "Mrs. May?"

"Do you hear running water?" Montana asked when there was no response from inside. "I hope it's not flooding."

"Better go see." Steele strode across the rustic bed-sitting room toward the bathroom. Montana trailed behind him, seeing too late the artfully discarded trail of intimate apparel leading the way to the bathroom.

"Oh!" When Steele froze in the threshold, Montana careened into him, knocking him into the steam-filled room, where a statuesque redhead stood beneath the shower spray.

She smiled at the sight of Steele. "It's about time. I was getting tired of waiting. Be a love and come wash my back."

The guest, who couldn't see Montana behind Steele, clearly assumed the two of them were alone.

Steele appeared nonplussed.

"Glad to see you got the shower working, Mrs. May."

"I told you earlier when I invited you up for a drink, it's Charmaine."

"Charmaine, have you met Montana Blackstone, Black Creek's owner? We were in a meeting when I got the call, and since her guests' comfort is of paramount importance, she wanted to follow up personally."

There was an abrupt silence as the water was turned off. "Well, now, isn't that above and beyond?"

As he spoke, Steele had moved back into the main room. Montana didn't know quite what to do when, seconds later, the redhead appeared, artfully draped in a towel that she held together with both hands.

"Pleased to meet you, Mrs. May." Montana automatically extended her hand.

The woman laughed. "Excuse me if I don't shake. I wouldn't want to lose my towel, now, would I?"

"I'll have Guest Services send you down a robe."

"How kind." The woman's eyes all but licked Steele from head to toe. "Rain check on the drink?"

"Anytime the bar's open," Steele said easily.

Judging by her frown, it was clearly not the answer the woman was hoping for.

As they drove back to the ranch house, Montana was silent.

"Does that sort of thing happen often?"

"I haven't been here long enough to know 'often.' I would have been more surprised if it never happened."

"No one working here has ever mentioned it."

"It's not an easy topic to broach. Some of your hands are basically shy. Zeb didn't know how to handle it."

"And you did."

"Yep. And I created a ranch policy."

"Without consulting *me?*"

"Beg your pardon, but it seems you've got more than enough on your plate."

"Don't even *try* to preempt me, Steele. I want to be apprised of everything that goes on here at Black Creek. And I don't want Black Creek known as the place where lonely widows can get lucky."

"Then I suggest you make sure none of the massage therapists you hire have other ideas."

She gasped. "Everyone I hire will be a professional."

He caught her arm. "It's simple male-female dynamics, Montana. It's bound to happen, so it's better to have the staff prepared to handle it."

"Right." Montana jerked her arm free. "Because we're a perfect example of what happens when there's no policy in place."

"But we *are* quite a team."

"Steele, you've never been a team player in your life. You have no idea of the meaning."

Montana had steamed out of the cart and into the house without another word. Better to leave her alone to get over her snit, Steele figured.

He ought to finish up his findings, file his Midas report, and get the hell out of here, except he was having too damn much fun. And Montana needed him more than she knew, for she was in an extremely vulnerable position: that no-man's-land where the turn of a card meant either a huge win or the loss of everything.

He'd been playing the game long enough to know the rules inside out, both official and unofficial. He knew how to stack the deck if need be. Although he never cheated, he always played to win. And if he won this time, Montana and Black Creek won as well.

He waited for a decent interval of time to pass before he went looking for Montana.

He knew her suite was on the ground floor at the back, with its own private courtyard. Vines almost obscured the narrow wrought-iron gateway. He stepped into the shadow-draped courtyard, where a string of white minilights illuminated a planting near the sunken hot tub.

Montana clearly didn't believe in drawing her drapes. He watched her inside, and from the stiff way she was moving, he guessed she was still pissed at him. He smiled, imagining how he might make it up to her. Before he could make his move, the French doors opened and Montana appeared in a midnight-blue bathrobe. She had a towel in one hand and a brandy snifter in the other.

Instinctively he stepped farther back into the shadows. She removed the hot tub cover, dropped her robe, and before he could fully enjoy the gilding of moonlight on her alabaster skin, she slid into the water. A touch of a switch, the soft hum of the pump, and the water surface frothed with bubbles.

Montana gave a long sigh of pleasure as she felt the hot water envelop her. She leaned her head back on the rim of the tub and stared up at the sky. Such a vast unknown space, mysterious and compelling at the same time. Not unlike her new foreman.

She knew he was good for Black Creek—just as she knew he was no good for her. He caught her off guard, kept her on edge, distracted her from matters at hand.

Yet she also needed his expertise. It was obvious things were under control due to his capable guidance. For so long, she'd felt all alone, shouldering the burden of Black Creek's future.

She loved the place, but knew she couldn't continue to operate it the way it had been in the past. Times had changed, along with the public's vacation needs.

And her needs. She released the cognac snifter to bob on the surface of the water, warming the liquor before she took a sip. The bouquet, the warmth, the taste—all stimulated her senses and filled her from the inside out, much the same as Steele.

She set the glass down behind her as the cognac tingled through her bloodstream and nested in that tangle of feminine mystery.

She was hot, on fire for Steele. She ran her hands across her breasts and imagined his talented fingertips massaging her nipples into urgent pleasure sensors, transmitting the aching need of fulfillment to her central core.

She reached between her legs and felt a responsive zing from her knee to her inner thigh.

She was so hot down there. Wet inside and out, alternately soothed and stimulated by the heated water and the magic of the pulsing jets. Her fingers wandered lower, between the slick folds, across the pearl of wisdom, to inside. She sighed in frustration. Her body wasn't fooled; it craved Steele's touch.

She slid lower in the tub and angled the pressure of the jet so it hit the tight knot in her shoulders where tension nestled, then dragged the jet's magic fingers back and forth across her back, then up and down the length of her spine to curve into her bottom. The sensation felt divine, familiar yet different, nowhere near Steele's magic touch.

She turned and let the water jet nuzzle her breasts and belly, and lower. So near and yet so far. Like Steele.

She widened her legs, narrowing the gap between the teasing blast of pressure and her throbbing emptiness. Muscular tension dissipated as sexual tension continued to build. She'd never felt this way, like a volcano was buried deep inside her, rumbling with discontent, a pressure valve screaming for release.

She sighed in longing, not really knowing what she longed for. What was this niggling discontent that she tried so hard to ignore over the years? This sense that, rich and full as her life was, something vital was missing?

She reached for her drink and felt the water jet's pulsing force meet and match her body's internal pulsing quest for more.

Drink forgotten, she slowly and deliberately repositioned herself. Gripping the edge of the tub for balance, she lifted her legs out of the water, exposed them to the cool night air.

As the water surge reached her, she caught her breath in

shock and delight at the hot rush of pleasure. She edged closer, forward and back, up and down, until her body and the water meshed in perfect sync.

The water rushed around her, through her, as she allowed its intense driving force to take over and direct her to self-satisfaction.

She could feel the water stream pummeling her female folds, different from any lover's touch. Creases and crevices swelled and opened in response to the teasing torture, till every particle of her cried out for release. She gripped the tub tighter, moved closer. The water's demanding, seeking touch filled her, till a rush of sensation swept clear through her. She let go of the edge, the force of the eruption sending her floating backward on a warm wave of ecstasy. She floated mindlessly on her back, staring skyward as tremors of delight lapped through her sated limbs.

Eventually she leaned back against the side and reached behind her for her drink. It wasn't where she had left it.

"I'm glad it was good for you." With an insufferable grin, Steele squatted down and placed the snifter in her outstretched hand.

Chapter Seven

Montana pounded back the cognac in a single swallow, gave him the empty glass, and pulled herself out of the hot tub, her movements as graceful as any dancer's.

Before she could reach for her towel, he draped it across her. He rubbed his chin across her damp shoulder, knowing most women liked the sensual rasp of a day's growth of whiskers. "I have great admiration for a woman who knows how to take care of herself."

She tossed her wet hair back, the ends slapping his cheek. "Even if it makes you redundant?"

"I like to think I have my uses."

"Obviously, so does Charmaine."

"I've handled my share of Charmaines."

"'Handled' being the operative word?"

When she grabbed her robe and headed inside, Steele followed.

She spun to face him, hands on hips. "These are my private living quarters."

"Very nice," he said, with an admiring glance. Another huge oil by Lamotia dominated one wall in a room done in a Southwest theme, where the white walls and white bed were offset by splashes of color so brilliant, it was almost violent. Turquoise. Red. Purple. Yellow. The space soothed and stimulated at the same time, an effect Steele bet was deliberate, for it matched Montana perfectly. A dim lamp in the far corner of the room offered the only illumination.

"I'm taking a shower."

"I can't wait to see what you do with the showerhead."

"I bet."

But she didn't move and neither did he.

"I've got a better idea," he said.

"Oh?"

"We both know the tub was only foreplay."

"And we both know I'm mad at you."

He flashed her his most engaging grin. "There's nothing like make-up sex."

When she didn't answer, he closed the distance between them. "We both know you need me."

"Like a fish needs a bicycle," Montana quipped.

"We both know you want me."

"Like a tooth wants a cavity."

He angled his body flush against hers. Her skin was moist and rosy pink, and he wanted nothing more than to lick her all over.

"I've never been jealous of a hot tub before tonight." It wasn't an easy admission, even for him.

She glanced up at him through a thick fringe of dark lashes. As her pupils dilated with excitement, he saw himself mirrored in their smoky depths. "Really."

"I wanted my tongue inside you, tracing your shape, lapping up your sweetness."

"Make up your mind if you're trying to seduce me or control me. You can't have both."

"I would never dream of controlling you."

"What about me controlling *you?*"

"I'm yours to command."

She eyed him in a sultry way that made him instantly hard and hot. "Take your clothes off and get into bed. I'll be right back."

Steele shed his jeans and shirt in record time, pushed down the virginal-white bedcover, and lay in wait.

He had been totally turned on tonight watching her in the tub, and it had taken every ounce of control not to join her. He stared at the ceiling, reminding himself that good things come to he who waits.

He didn't wait long before Montana appeared at his side looking like every man's fantasy. A body-hugging black bustier pushed her breasts up so they overflowed the narrow confines and her dark nipples spied on him. She wore killer black stilettos that made her long legs appear longer, sheathed in sheer black stockings held up by a garter belt.

"Baby!" He hoped his approving leer didn't look as goofy as he felt when he reached for her.

Her hand on his bare chest stopped him, her touch branding-iron hot. "You promised me control."

"And so far I'm not regretting it."

She stroked his aching, hard cock. "So it would appear. Now give me your hands."

"Why?" His eyes widened as she unwound a slim silk scarf from around her waist.

"Why do you think?"

God, she was making him crazy. He was trembling like a schoolboy. "If you tie me up, I won't be able to touch you."

"But you can watch." Slowly and deliberately, she wound the silk scarf around his wrists and lashed them to the headboard. Her tits all but fell out of her bustier as she bent over. If he wasn't bound, he'd grab them, bring them up to his mouth, and suckle like a hungry babe. His cock swelled at the prospect, throbbing with a fresh surge of blood.

"There." She stepped back to admire her handiwork.

He gave a gentle tug to his bonds. Not a lot of slack. Life on a ranch had taught her to tie a killer knot.

"You like to watch, don't you, Steele?"

"Who doesn't?"

She stood before him, enticing and magnificent. He could see the slight shadow of her pubic hair and, when she moved those long luscious legs, a tiny glimmer of her moist pink delights, like the inside of a seashell.

God, he'd never been so horny in his life. His cock stood at rigid attention.

"He wants you," Steele said. His pulse raced, his breath rose and fell in shallow pants as she approached the bed.

"What should we do about that?" She pressed her forefinger to her lips and pretended to ponder the situation.

"You're in control."

"An idea I quite like."

She pulled a peacock feather from a floral display. "Ticklish, Steele?"

"Nah," he said. Turned out he lied.

She played the feather across his nipples, under his armpits, down his side to his waist and he flinched, wondering where next, as she attacked the balls of his feet, his legs, then the particularly sensitive skin near his groin. She laughed when he rolled to one side, trying vainly to avoid her. When the feather tickled his sac, it felt like his cock was on fire.

"Enough, you got me! I *am* ticklish."

She leaned over him. "I'm just getting started."

He sucked in his breath as the soft, round overflow of her breasts brushed his chest. As she rubbed them back and forth he watched her nipples harden, her eyes half closed with a low growl of pleasure.

"Are you wet?" he said.

"Very."

"Show me."

She straddled him and tilted her hips, jutting her pelvis forward so her pubes tickled his abs and he could feel her heat searing him, racing through his bloodstream.

He could just see the faintest tease of pale pink moistness.

He wanted to touch her so bad.

Then, like something from a wet dream, she reached down and opened herself for his viewing pleasure. Pale pink deepened to luscious rose inside, her petals quivering in anticipation.

"Come up here," he said.

"You sure?" She pivoted her hips, rubbing herself against him. Then she dipped forward and offered him her breasts, pulling their plump roundness free of their confines.

He gulped them like a starving man, his tongue lashing and laving, eager lips shaping and sucking as her low murmurs of pleasure seared right through to his groin. He was afraid he might come right then and there.

She showed no mercy, dragging her breasts back and forth across his face and open mouth.

When she inched forward he could feel her heat, smell the musky scent of her arousal, and he couldn't plunge his tongue into her fast enough. No teasing tastes, just instant possession, fast and hard. She was sweeter and juicier than the choicest fruit, and after his initial guzzle he settled in to enjoy her. To allow her to control the pace, the speed, the depth.

She knelt above him, palming her exposed breasts, her eyes half shut, her breathing shallow as his tongue darted in and out, stimulating her to the orgasm he knew was about to hit.

He felt it before she did. First the tightening, then the initial shudder, just as he sucked her clit in a move that made her rear up with a strangled scream of pleasure.

"That beat your Jacuzzi?"

"It might." She was soft and pliant atop him as she shimmied back down his length. Her move reminded him of the exotic dancers he'd seen perform in Vegas, except this time he was the prop. And she was shamelessly using him for her own pleasure.

She slowly dragged her hot pussy the length of his aching cock. Her wet heat enveloped him for a brief second before it was gone, and she slid off the end of the bed.

"Hey!" His voice was so husky he barely recognized it as his. "Where are you going?"

"I'll be back." She leaned over and kissed him. He knew she could taste herself on his lips from the way she licked him clean.

The sight of her beautiful bare ass was his to enjoy as she walked away. Seconds later she was back, dragging a cheval mirror into place at the foot of the bed.

"Can you see?"

"Oh, yeah. I see the most sexually frustrated male on the planet."

She eyed his throbbing cock. "He does look like he needs to be put out of his misery. Soon."

Steele tugged at his bonds. "Untie me."

"I don't think so."

She brought over the bottle of cognac and drizzled the cool liquid across his hot skin. Then she leaned over and lapped the liquor from his belly button. His groin tightened; his legs actually quivered. He rolled from side to side.

"Montana, you're killing me."

"Mmmmm, good." She looked up at him, licking her lips. "Want a taste?"

When she kissed him his senses exploded from the heady flavor of the liquor, underlying her sweet heat.

Just when he thought he couldn't take a minute more of her teasing, she straddled him again, backward this time.

She took hold of his cock and ran her hands up his length from root to tip, hand over hand. He could see it all in the mirror. Her loving caress, her breasts spilling above the bustier, the contrast of white skin against black lace. Her hands on him were torture, one tickling his balls, one on his cock.

Then she shifted so she could rub her damp pussy up and down his length, moistening him with the dew of her arousal. She pivoted so his tip nuzzled her clit. She was pulsing, throbbing, or was that him? He was lost in a whirl of sensation. The sight of Montana, the lingering taste of her and the cognac, her hot, hungry lower lips teased him to madness while her ass bobbed up and down as if she were already riding him.

When she finally lowered herself onto his aching hardness, he had to bite his lip to keep from exploding into her.

Montana rode him slowly at first, her heat gloving him, loving him. Gradually she increased the pace till she became a woman possessed, the mirror positioned so she could watch him watching her.

It was impossible not to hit her G-spot at this angle, and he knew he'd hit the jackpot when he felt a rush of hot liquid drowning him. He couldn't tear his gaze from the mirror. As

Montana rode him she fondled her breasts and touched herself where they were joined.

Two more orgasms ripped through her, and he was congratulating himself on his control when she reached down past his balls, found that special sweet spot with her slick, slippery fingers, then slid her baby finger up inside him.

He exploded inside her with a hoarse cry of surrender that she met and matched with her own, rearing up almost off of him before she collapsed in a limp heap.

Neither of them were capable of movement or speech for several long minutes; then she finally reached up to untie him.

When he grabbed her and pulled her close, her head pillowed on his chest, she wrapped one leg atop his with a sexy slither of sheer stockinged leg.

Montana woke in a tangle of sweat-dampened limbs. When she stirred, she felt Steele's hold on her tighten. He stroked her bare arm while she lay there wondering how to extricate herself.

What on earth had come over her? It felt like someone else had taken over her body. Not only would Steele think that was what she was really like, she'd have a heck of a time getting back to any sort of professional standing now.

She'd quite liked being in control, having all the power. She simply needed to transfer that into their workday.

Starting now. She sat up.

"Steele, you can't spend the night."

"Is that the boss talking? Or the woman intent on keeping her distance?"

"You like to push people, don't you?"

"Fast as you put up the boundaries, I'll be tearing them down."

She gave him her haughtiest look. "I'm going to have a shower. I want you gone by the time I get back."

Moving so fast it was a blur, he lunged across the bed, grabbed her hands in both of his, and pinned her to the bed.

"Maybe it's my turn to have control."

"I'm done playing games. I'm tired."

"Who's playing?" He loomed atop her, dark and dangerous, and despite herself Montana felt a fresh stirring of excitement. She might be no match for his physical strength, but she had other resources to call on.

"Bully!"

He sipped the insult from her lips, swallowed it like it didn't exist, and Montana melted beneath him. She kissed him back, devoured him with an insatiable hunger, until she felt him release her.

He drew back, ran his hands down her, and then slowly rolled to his feet and reached for his clothes. "Just because I'm leaving doesn't mean you won this hand. And next time we're together, be warned. It'll be one of *my* fantasies we play out."

He left and Montana rolled over, her skin still burning from his touch, as she wondered just what sort of fantasies intrigued Steele.

Never let it be said that he didn't know when to let the other player win a few, Steele thought, whistling as he let himself out of the courtyard. Adrenaline thrummed through him, a hit of that after-sex energy Montana had boasted about.

He felt like Superman, invincible, a man of steel. He was still grinning when he reached the bunkhouse.

"Well, aren't you looking like the cat who swallowed the canary," Zeb said. "It must have gone well tonight."

Steele froze and put on a neutral face. "What do you mean?"

Zeb gave him a look. "I mean with the horny guest over at Spur."

"Mrs. May." Steele chuckled. "Montana was less than impressed, but I think everyone is clear on the situation."

"I don't know if you've done foreman work before," Zeb said. "And I don't all that much care. As long as you're good for Black Creek."

"I try."

Alone in his room, Steele booted up his laptop and scanned his in-progress report. Something was nagging him, and as he read what he had written so far, he realized it wasn't so much what was in the report as the fact that he wasn't yet ready to e-mail it. He made a few more notes and put the computer away. Maybe things would look clearer after a good night's sleep.

Unfortunately, they looked even worse in the light of day. As Steele inspected the fences the next morning, he frowned. His job at Black Creek was done, and he knew it. So why was he dragging his heels? He had everything he needed to file that damn report and move on, but he kept finding new excuses not to. That had never happened before.

His phone rang and he checked the caller ID. "I told you not to call me here," he said.

"What's the holdup?"

"No holdup," Steele said curtly.

"It's never taken you this long before."

"Things are more complicated than I originally thought. Usually the business owner hires me, and I don't need to sneak around behind their back."

"Face it, Steele, you like sneaking around. I need that report ASAP. I'm meeting with my board next week."

"And you'll have it. I still wonder how you got Helen on *your* side. She seems genuinely fond of her daughter-in-law."

The smug voice said, "I told you it would be no problem." A pause. "Should I be worried about my investment?"

"It'll all be in the report."

Steele hung up and leaned on the fence post, surveying the sprawling acres of Black Creek. He wanted the new resort and spa to succeed as much as Montana did. Which meant he had to get busy.

Chapter Eight

Steele Hardt was dangerous. The man had Montana doing and saying things she never normally would. And, ridiculous as it was, she actually resented the way his presence was lightening her workload. He was more than capable of dealing with whatever arose, which left her free to concentrate on the myriad of details necessary to pull the resort together.

"Any regrets about taking Steele on?"

She started as Helen broke into her thoughts, then realized Helen's version of taking Steele on in no way meshed with hers.

"Some," she said shortly. *More personal than professional.*

"Oh, dear," Helen said, with a frown. "I hoped you two had come to some sort of understanding."

"I doubt there will ever be any understanding Steele," Montana said. "This whole undertaking seems a very strange gig for him. You know how I hate it when things don't make sense."

"But Zeb said he has the respect of all the men and things are running much smoother on that side."

Montana nodded. "I put a lot of store in what Zeb thinks. If he says Steele being here is a good thing, that's good enough for me."

"Have you noticed a difference in Zeb lately?" Helen asked.

"Not really, why?"

"Oh, no special reason. You will let me know if there's anything I can do, won't you?"

Giving Helen any sort of simple task would be far more work than seeing to it herself. "Thanks, Helen. I appreciate that."

"Do you ever think that if Charlie were here, he'd know just exactly what to do?"

Montana gave Helen a look. "No, Helen. I never think that."

"Me either," Helen said with a sigh. "It's a shame."

Montana knew she was taking a risk by hiring her chef before the resort's dining room was even finished, but she needed the best and she needed the buzz.

Sitting across the desk from her was the best: Daniel Perri.

Temperamental, egotistical, and enormously talented. Most important, he was young and eager to prove himself. They'd had numerous phone conversations prior to his arrival and the fact that he was willing to come out and see the place meant he was seriously considering the move. Unfortunately, she needed him more than he needed her, and he knew it.

They'd had a good day so far, and Montana was feeling confident. Daniel liked the fact that he could design and outfit the kitchen to meet his needs, as well as have total creative carte blanche with the menu.

"I don't want tried, true, and safe," Montana said. "I want to raise the bar, to be the resort others emulate."

"No easy task," Daniel said.

"I believe it's achievable. The question is, are you the one who can make it happen?"

"Your success is my success."

"And vice versa."

"I have only one concern."

She leaned forward. "Tell me."

"If, as you maintain, Black Creek is a can't-lose proposition, why is Midas here?"

She frowned. "Midas?"

"You would know him as Steele Hardt. Midas is his nickname—the man with the golden touch."

"Steele's my ranch foreman. What's this about gold?"

Daniel laughed. "You really don't know?"

"Know what?"

"He first became famous for his skill with the cards, till he retired from that life. Now he troubleshoots floundering businesses—either euthanizes them or turns them around."

"You must be mistaken. My mother-in-law hired Steele as foreman."

"Then you need to find out who hired him as a consultant. I'm guessing someone might not want to see you succeed."

Montana drew a determined breath. "I have every intention of succeeding. Now, are you in or are you out?"

And so began the delicate art of negotiation, during which Montana didn't push as hard as she normally would, distracted by this latest information.

As soon as she and Daniel had hammered out a deal, which included his buying shares in the resort, she called someone to drive him to the airport, turned on her computer, and Googled Steele Hardt.

Dusk had crept in without her noticing by the time she finally turned off her computer. Did she have a surprise for Mr. Hardt.

Steele couldn't leave until the overgrown airstrip was paved. At least, that's what he told himself. "And after that?"

"After that, what?" Zeb asked.

Steele started. "Sorry, thinking out loud."

Zeb just nodded. "Helps to clear the head sometimes."

If only his head were so easily cleared. Images of Montana kept drifting through, muddying his thoughts. He was determined to give her something to remember him by. He smiled to himself in anticipation. She liked control, that much was obvious. What else might she like that she didn't even know she liked?

Zeb cleared his throat and seemed to be waiting. "Something on your mind, Zeb?"

"In a manner of speaking."

"So spit it out."

"I gather you've had a fair bit of success with the ladies over the years."

Steele bit back a smile. "You could say that."

"What's the best way to make amends? Say you do something that seems a good idea, then turns out it really isn't."

"You care to be a little more specific?"

"The black widows. They're difficult ladies to figure out, but you seem to be getting along okay with Montana, after a shaky start."

"You could say that. But I get the feeling she's not the black widow we're talking about"

Zeb let out a pent-up breath. "Last night, after dinner, I kissed Miss Helen. Something I've been wanting to do for a long time."

"How did she take it?"

"Slapped my face good."

"Not the reaction you were hoping for."

"I've been here too many years watching her make a fool of herself with the youngsters. Figured it was time she had a taste of a real man."

"Do you care for her, Zeb?"

"More than life itself."

"Well, that's the kind of stuff women like to hear. After that usually comes the kissing part."

"Hard business, figuring out the fairer sex."

"It is that."

"Hey, Zeb!" Don called out. "Miss Montana wants to see you up at the big house."

"Okey dokey." Zeb sent Steele a look. "Any idea what the boss lady wants?"

"Your guess is as good as mine."

Montana glanced to where Zeb stood across the desk from her, fingering the rim of the Stetson he held and looking as if he'd rather be anyplace but here. She cut to the chase. "Tell me Steele's not working out and I'll get rid of him."

"No reason to be doing that, from what I can see."

"You mean to tell me he's doing a credible job as foreman?"

"Can't fault the man, Montana. I was skeptical at first on account of Miss Helen hiring him, but having him here is making a difference in all the right ways."

"All right, then," Montana said. It would be better for all concerned if Steele left under his own steam, anyway. "I'd like you to send one of the hands to the airport to pick up a visitor this afternoon. The man's name is Murdoch."

"Montana, Zeb just told me you're bringing in a consultant named Murdoch. I really don't think that's necessary."

"Why, Helen? Because you hired Steele in that exact same capacity and lied to me about it?"

Helen cast her eyes downward. "I was never comfortable with the lie. All I want is what's best for you and for the ranch."

"Perfect," Montana said. "I believe that bringing Murdoch to the ranch is for the best."

Helen slanted her a look that perhaps saw too much. "I do hope you know what you're doing, my dear."

So did she. So did she.

Where the hell was Montana hiding out? By the end of the following day, Steele bit down hard on his frustration. He knew she was on the ranch someplace, and her whereabouts seemed a deliberate game of cat and mouse. He'd find out where she was supposed to be, only to arrive and find she'd vanished. Sometimes he could even detect lingering traces of her perfume, as if she'd left the room only moments earlier.

After chasing her in vain the better part of the day, he was totally out of sorts. He'd taken his frustration out on the ranch hands, till eventually Zeb had told him to go cool off.

He'd done just that, got himself under control and headed over to the ranch house for one more attempt to find Montana. He arrived just as the front door opened and out she stepped, cool as a cucumber.

"There you are," he said with a growl.

"Steele," she said sweetly. "Just the man I'm looking for." She stepped aside. "I believe you know Murdoch."

Murdoch the Magician! Steele's blood hit the boiling point. No wonder she'd been avoiding him.

A beefy hand was extended his way. "Good to see you again, Hardt. I could hardly believe my ears when Montana told me you'd been hired on as foreman. Giving your brother a run for his job?"

Steele reluctantly shook the other man's hand. "It never hurts to remember where we came from." His words were a deliberate dig at the other man and they both knew it. Murdoch was a business consultant who had rung the death knell for several companies, after which Steele had stepped in and resurrected them. Steele had been freely quoted in the press, stating it was easier to kill than to resuscitate. Murdoch hadn't seen the truth or the humor in Steele's words, and the gloves had come off.

Folks who didn't know better might have thought they were in competition. Opposition was more like it. Steele liked Murdoch even less than he liked the man's business tactics.

"Well, if you'll excuse us, Murdoch and I have a lot of ground to cover before dark," Montana said.

"Just a minute. I want to talk to you a sec." Steele caught hold of her arm harder than he'd intended.

"Do you mind waiting in the truck?" she asked Murdoch. "This won't take long."

"What the hell is he doing here?" Steele said the second the other man was gone.

"More to the point," Montana said sweetly, "what the hell are you doing here, Midas?"

She sashayed off to the truck, leaving him staring at her dust.

Montana was still mentally congratulating herself as she washed her face and brushed her teeth. The look on Steele's face had been worth every penny she had spent on bringing Murdoch to the ranch for the day.

First thing tomorrow, she'd tell Steele his services were no longer required. Him and all his lip service about teamwork . . . Steele's self-serving team of one!

She had just climbed into bed and turned out the light when she heard a faint sound that didn't belong, a kind of swishing noise. Instantly alert, she held her breath and listened but didn't hear it again. Still, the hairs on the back of her neck prickled as she lay stiff limbed and silent.

Montana trusted her instincts enough to know she'd never fall asleep until she ensured all was in order. She flicked on the lamp and started to sit up, only to be grabbed from behind. Before she choked out a muffled scream, a gag was stuffed into her mouth, a blanket was tossed over her head, and she was carried through the courtyard, kicking and thrashing.

Steele—it had to be him! She heard a muttered oath as her wild kick connected with some part of male anatomy. Rough hands bound her ankles before she was hefted, stomach down, across the saddleless back of a horse. She lay trussed up and uncomfortable as her captor mounted up behind her and the horse started to move.

What if it wasn't Steele? What if it was some kidnapper, mistakenly thinking the black widows were flush and holding her for ransom?

Don't think like that. It had to be Steele, engrossed in some warped control game.

And here she was, getting turned on despite herself. The rhythm of the horse's stride added fuel to the cool fingers of desert night air penetrating the rough wool of the blanket.

It took some doing, but she managed to spit out her gag. "At least let me sit astride," she said loudly.

She heard a masculine chuckle.

"I doubted anything would keep you quiet for long. We're almost there."

A large masculine hand caressed her backside, and she could feel the heat of his touch through the thin silk of her short nightie. She rolled from side to side in an attempt to avoid his touch.

"Careful," he said, grabbing a fistful of her nightgown. "You might fall off."

"Fat lot you'd care." She changed tactics. "Can you take the blanket off my head? I'm claustrophobic."

"In good time."

"I think I'm going to throw up," she added. "I can't breathe."

The wool blanket was scratchy beneath her and as the horse moved it rubbed against her breasts, causing her nipples to swell and harden.

Bringing Murdoch into the mix had obviously riled Steele good, to the point where he'd go to extremes to wrest control. Clearly she'd gotten to him in ways she'd never planned.

She felt him bring the horse to a stop and dismount. Using her hands for leverage, Montana wriggled off backward. With her ankles bound, she had no balance and wound up flat on her back with the blanket tangled around her. She clawed at the covering, trying to get it off her face, before she was scooped up like a limp bag of straw, her arms imprisoned at her sides.

She heard boot heels against wooden planking, then a door being kicked open. He'd brought her to the old ranch cabin, now used to shelter any hands who found themselves working too far from the bunkhouses.

She was deposited on the hard seat of a wooden straight-back chair with her hands tied behind her.

"Enough, Steele. You've made your point. I concede to your masculine strength and mastery."

The blanket was lifted off from behind, but before she had time to do more than blink, a blindfold swiftly replaced it.

Montana licked her dry lips and forced herself to stay calm. Steele would soon tire of the game. He wasn't dangerous. At least not in the physical sense.

"May I have a drink of water, please?"

If she could distract him, get to her feet, slip her hands off the back of the chair . . .

As if her thoughts were being read, her ankles were untied, cool fingers on her bare knees easing her legs apart—and each ankle was lashed to a chair leg. When he stroked her inner thigh lightly, Montana felt a rush of excitement flood through her. Her bare tush rested against the wooden seat. How much of the rest of her was exposed? Was the dark shadow of her pubic hair visible through the thin silk? Could he tell she was getting wet? Perhaps the silk was damp where it brushed her. She tried to press her legs together, but her bonds prevented it.

When a cool glass rim brushed her lips, she tilted her head back and tasted champagne.

"My favorite."

"Nothing but the best." When she was done, he took away the glass and traced the shape of her champagne-damp lips with one finger.

Her tongue licked him and then she sucked hard, pulling his finger deep into her mouth. Suddenly the temperature in the cabin rose several degrees. He ran his other hand through her loose hair and caressed her scalp, which prickled in response.

"What's this all about?" she asked.

"Isn't that obvious? I'm getting you out of my system."

She wished she could see him, stare deep into his eyes and gauge the truth. She tossed back her head in challenge. "Ever think it might backfire?"

"All the time."

"Then why stay?"

"I've been asking myself the very same thing."

She felt his hand clamp her breast and quivered at the way he molded her breast to his palm, kneading the nipple into a tight and aching bud.

"You're here because you've never met a woman like me before."

"You're too headstrong to recognize your vulnerability." His words held a mocking note.

"Is that what this is about? Proving me vulnerable?"

She heard him circle the chair as they talked, no doubt observing her from all angles. He touched her freely, trailed his fingers over her face to her neck and shoulders.

Did his touch have more power than before, or was it simply that she couldn't see him, couldn't touch him back?

When he raked his nails the length of her bare arms, she sighed in spite of herself. Blindfolded, it seemed all other senses were heightened.

Everyplace he touched, new nerve endings sprang to life. The impact was subtle, highly erotic.

And she'd never give him the satisfaction he was looking for. "I like what you're doing. The way you're making me feel."

"Oh? Why?"

"I'm not accustomed to the passive role. It's a nice change." From performing on stage to performing in the bedroom, she'd always taken the lead. This was the first time she'd felt totally free to simply feel.

"I didn't think you'd like it," Steele said. "You thrive on control."

"I'm comfortable taking control," she corrected.

He brushed against her, his denim-clad thigh rough against her bare leg. She was getting off on the contrast, and so was he. He loomed above her, one leg on either side of her, and she licked her lips in anticipation, wondering what he might do next.

He took hold of her nightie at the neckline and pulled it toward him. He must have cut it with a knife, for it floated away from her.

"How about giving me control?" he suggested.

"What other choice do I have?"

"Wise lady. Don't even try to bluff your hand."

"How can I? You're holding all the aces."

"I am, aren't I?" Suddenly his touch changed from gentle

to urgent. He kissed her hard, but his lips didn't linger to play with hers. She felt the lap of his tongue as it laved her breastbone, between her breasts, then across her belly to the top of her thighs.

She tensed, took a breath, then forced herself to relax. She envisioned him kneeling before her, his dark head between her legs. She started at the first brush of his tongue on that soft, vulnerable flesh and felt her insides respond with a melting warmth that spread pleasurably through her inner core.

He pushed her legs farther apart, open for his viewing pleasure. She felt the heat of his gaze, followed by the coolness of his breath as he blew on her exposed female petals.

It wasn't easy, but Montana forced herself to remain still.

"If only you could see yourself the way I see you. Rosy and moist with anticipation."

"You excite me," she said.

"Show me." She heard the sound of him getting to his feet, followed by the loud rasp as he unzipped his jeans.

Seconds later, the velvet tip of his penis danced across her lips.

Chapter Nine

"Are you comfortable?" Helen reached to tuck a second pillow beneath Zeb's head.

"Don't fuss," he said.

She leaned over and kissed him. "First time I've heard it called that."

He flushed a half dozen shades of crimson, recovered, and cleared his throat. "Just so you know, I'll be monopolizing your spare time from here on in."

"Why, Zeb! I never knew you cared."

He avoided her teasing gaze. "It tried my patience, waiting for you to sow your wild oats. Figured I'd better have my say for once."

"I'm glad you did. I was getting pretty exhausted from trying to make you jealous."

He blanched. "That's what you were about? Making me jealous?"

She gave a smug smile and rolled over so that she was sprawled across him. "You have to admit it worked."

"You think so, do you?"

She gave a gentle tug at his chest hairs. "I'm all for testing that Viagra you have—not that you've needed it so far."

He cradled her gently, and Helen felt something inside of her melt when he said, "You make me feel as if I've only just started to really live."

She blinked away a mist blurring her vision. "Promise you'll always be there for me."

"I promise."

"Can we keep this to ourselves a little longer? I just want Montana to get the resort on firm footing before I tell her we're leaving."

"Of course."

As Steele teased her, Montana teased him back, keeping her lips firmly shut. His velvet tip rolled across her cheekbones, her chin, then back up to nuzzle her waiting lips.

She opened the slightest bit, exposed her tongue to trace the tiny eye, then expand to broader, sweeping strokes. He sucked in his breath as her exploration grew to encompass the entire head. She sheathed her teeth with her lips and formed a small, round open invitation with her mouth. In and out he slid, just the tip, careful not to insert his full length. She could hear the acceleration in his breathing, its increased speed matching the pace with which he explored her.

He threaded his fingers through her hair, urged her head back, and she brought her tongue into play, sword-fighting him.

"Jesus, Montana." He stopped abruptly and pulled out, his grip on her gentling. She licked her lips. They were hot, swollen, and tingling, just like her inner lips.

"Now that you've captured me, what do you plan to do with me?" Her voice husked with sexual desire.

"What should I do with you?"

"Oral pleasure would be nice."

"Even bound, you refuse to be passive."

"Don't you know? The passive one ultimately holds the power."

"I'm learning that."

She felt something light and gauzy wisp across her face and her breasts, and raised her face to arch her neck, like a cat craving further petting. She guessed it was a silk scarf, given the way it slithered down her arms and across her thighs, its touch more fleeting than any ghostly lover.

Montana grew impatient. She raised one foot, then the other, till she managed to rock her chair from side to side.

He grabbed her shoulders and held her still. "Don't do that. You'll fall."

She leaned forward till her lips brushed his. "I trust you to catch me."

"Liar. You don't trust anyone."

She pulled back, caught in her own lie. "I did once."

"What happened?"

"He died," Montana said softly.

"Charlie?"

She shook her head and felt the emptiness that resulted from him moving away.

"What's the matter," she taunted. "Jealous of a ghost?"

He was back before her in an instant. "There are no ghosts," he said, low voiced. "Only you and me."

His hands gripped her legs hard as he knelt and buried his face in her soft, waiting warmth.

At the first touch of his lips, Montana exhaled on a breathy sigh. She leaned her head against the chair back and focused solely on that burning central core of pleasure, on the sensations wrought by the magic of Steele's tongue and lips. He traced her internal shape, laving it, lapping its softness, coaxing the sweet flood of dampness to enhance his own moist warmth. He murmured his approval as he sipped and licked and drank her essence, encouraging the tremors of delight that continued to ripple through her from the inside out.

"Touch my breasts."

He reached up and caressed that neglected part of her. They fairly leapt into his palms and as he molded her nipples into swelling buds of delight, she felt another jolt of sensation to the hidden pearl of her womanhood.

She rocked her pelvis slightly, increasing the pressure of his tongue, then sobbed aloud at the first wave of release.

The sensation continued to expand and swell as he twirled his tongue around her engorged pearl. When a second, more intense orgasm hit, she gasped and rose off her seat in an involuntary spasm. Her limbs quivered in the aftermath while she gasped for air.

He ran his hands the length of her bound legs from knee to thigh and back to knee. She could feel the ridge of calluses on his hands, followed by the delicious rasp of his nails.

Not seeming content with his efforts so far, he continued to tweak and tease, his tongue probing her pulsing opening. She thrashed in her seat, unsure if she could endure further torture as he caressed her with his chin, rubbing it against the softness of her inner thighs, the day's growth of whiskers a delicious abrading to her limp and sated state. She clenched her hands, fingertips tingling with the need to freely touch and torture him as he touched her.

"Untie my hands."

"All in good time."

He rose and kissed her on the lips. She could taste the commingling of their flavors, a heady aphrodisiac that further inflamed her.

"Untie me so I can touch you," she murmured against him.

"What?" he said teasingly. "This from the woman who kept me bound and helpless while she pleasured herself?"

"I let you watch."

"There are other senses to indulge." His tongue stroked her lower lip. "Taste yourself."

Montana quivered, parted her lips. Not only did Steele know how to charge her battery physically, his game was more far-reaching; getting her off on the unknown. His breath mingled with hers as he kneaded the tight muscles of her calves.

"And you feel me touching you."

She pushed out her bottom lip in a pout. "I have no freedom to touch you." As she spoke she managed to brush his arm with her breast, a caress of wash-worn denim on her skin. She heard his breath catch and redoubled her efforts till he moved away.

"Even bound, you manage to have your way."

She laughed, anticipating what he might do next.

When a glass of champagne found its way to her lips she sipped eagerly, but before she'd drunk her fill he tipped the glass away from her. She squealed as cold liquid hit her skin, trickled slowly from her shoulders, across her breasts and belly, to her hips and the tops of her legs.

"My, my," he said. "You seem to have spilled your drink."

His tongue on her skin was like softened sandpaper as he licked the liquid from her shoulders. He made his way slowly and carefully from her collarbone to her Eve's trough, his tongue a languid instrument of arousal.

Down her breastbone, with a brief detour to taste her breasts and suck her nipples.

Instantly a flutter of arousal ignited in her belly and seeped lower—flames of desire fanned by Steele's tongue massage and the fact that she had no control over what happened next.

"Take me to bed," she said.

"Now, there's an idea."

She hardly dared believe it when her feet were finally freed, then her hands. She flexed her ankles to make sure she had full circulation, ripped off the blindfold, and ran out the cabin door and into the black of night. The fact that she'd been blindfolded gave her an advantage, for her eyes needed no time to adjust. Plus she was familiar with this area. Steele's horse stood off to the side and she scrambled to mount, took hold of the reins, and dug in her heels—all for nothing. The horse refused to move.

"Nice try, Lady Godiva." Steele reached her side, quite unconcerned about her escape attempt. She dug her heels into the horse's flanks one last time, then threw down the reins in disgust.

"Do you always play to win?" she said.

"What gambler doesn't?" He tugged her into his waiting arms, bare skin against muscle-encased denim.

She looked up, wishing she could see his eyes, read something in his expression, but his face was in shadow. "You owe me a nightdress. It was silk."

"I always pay my debts." He scooped her into his arms and returned to the cabin, where he bolted the door.

The bed was ready and waiting.

Montana wasn't.

As soon as he put her down she crossed the room and helped herself to more champagne. Steele followed.

"You're supposed to fall in love with your captor, not flee from him."

"I told you I didn't want to be restrained. I wanted to touch you as you were touching me."

"I told you, all in good time."

"I'm impatient."

"It scares you, doesn't it? Not having control."

"Don't analyze me, Steele. You're the one who ripped me from my warm bed."

"Analyze the fact that I can't keep my hands off of you." She turned slowly, stunned by the admission. "I'm guessing that scares you."

"Damn right. I never get involved with people I work with."

She shrugged. "Forget the work part. We both have our fears. I know that by expanding Black Creek, it becomes too much for one person to run and I have to relinquish control."

"I fear how much I want you. The more I taste you, the more I have you, the more I crave you. It's like trying to quench your thirst with ocean water. Impossible. Ultimately deadly. It's like an addiction. There's never enough."

"Then I suggest you take me back, before your addiction gets the best of you." She picked up the blanket she'd arrived in and kicked aside her ruined nightdress. "Don't forget. Silk."

"Like your skin." He trailed a hand across her bare back, fingers leaving a trail of fire. She flipped the blanket over her shoulders like a cape, as if it had the power to smother her feelings.

Steele opened the cabin door and ushered her through. Outside, she easily mounted his waiting horse and moved forward to make room behind her. Yet as soon as he was in place, some unnamed instinct made her spin around so that her whole body faced him. It wasn't an easy maneuver, but she made it appear effortless.

"Were you an acrobat in a former life?"

"Close. A dancer."

"That explains a lot." As he reached around her for the reins, Steele recalled the way she had slithered across him the other night while he was tied to the bed.

And now she sat in his arms, her hands on his shoulders for balance, the heat of her touch reminding him they had unfinished business.

The moon lavished silver gilt on her bare legs, snug against his.

"You sure you're comfortable?" His voice came out clogged in his throat.

Her soft laughter knotted his insides. "More comfortable than you."

Her fingers curled in his crotch to cradle the stirring bulge in his jeans. Teasingly she ran her fingers along the seam, then walked her hands up and tucked her fingertips beneath the waistband of his jeans. He sucked his breath through his teeth as her fingers burrowed lower, grazed the tip of his straining cock.

"Don't you wish you'd untied me sooner?"

"I wish I'd taken you earlier." He was deliberately crude, hoping it would deter her, but it seemed to have the opposite effect. She unzipped his jeans and, with a soft coo of delight, freed his swollen length.

"Stop it, Montana."

"Stop what? This?" She licked her palm and slicked it

across his tip. "Or this?" She made a ring of thumb and middle finger, to glide his length with precise and maddening slowness.

The blanket slid lower as they rode. Thank goodness their horse knew the way, for Steele couldn't tear his gaze from the shadow of her feminine triangle. As if reading his thoughts, she edged forward till they met, and he found his cock enfolded in the teasing warmth of her lower lips.

"Oh, my." She did a killer side-to-side shift so he nudged her clit and he felt a fresh flood of heated dampness surround him.

He bit his lower lip hard. He hadn't been this close to losing it, ever. The horse's gait beneath them, compounded by a naked Montana all but riding his dick . . . Steele exhaled with a shaky breath.

"Having fun?" he asked.

"Starting to." She wriggled even closer till he was nearly in her, straining toward her heat. She raised and lowered her hips, using her legs for leverage and holding him for balance.

He stifled a groan. It was the most highly erotic sensation ever. Her moist pussy nudging him, attempting to swallow him, her eyes half closed in concentration while her breasts bobbed perkily before him. He tapped the horse's flanks with his heels and watched her breasts dance as he slid inside her.

"Oh, yes!" Her grip tightened. Her internal muscles clenched around him but couldn't hold him. She was so wet, melting hot, melting him, as he slid in and out of her in time to the horse's gait.

She leaned forward, clutched his shoulders, and gave his

neck a gentle nip. Her breasts hugged him as she raised herself up and down, increasing the friction of their joining. She pivoted so her clit got full-on attention from his cock, along with the rest of her. He'd never had such a ride. Darkness enveloped them, all sensation centered on the immediate here and now of the woman in his arms and the animal beneath them, surrounded by the smell and feel of hot, raw primitive sex.

He let go of the reins, trusting the horse knew his way to food and warmth. He needed to touch Montana everywhere, to be reassured he was making her as crazy as she was making him. From the way she moaned and clutched him, her nails digging into first his waist, then his shoulders and arms, she was having the ride of her life.

He pushed her hair back, cupped her face in his hands, and concentrated everything on a kiss as hot as their joining. A kiss that told her he owned her. At least for tonight.

She kissed him back with an energy that stole his breath and all but stopped his heart, as he tried to focus on making everything last.

He felt rising heat and swelling pressure, just as her body surged with a massive orgasm. Powerless to fight its force, he let himself be carried right along with her.

Chapter Ten

Montana rolled over to sunlight streaming across her face, and bounded from bed. She never slept in. And what was that noise? It sounded like a plane approaching the landing strip, a sound she hadn't heard since Charlie's time.

She dressed quickly, grabbed a cup of coffee, and stepped out onto the front porch, smack into a buzzing undercurrent of activity and excitement that she'd never heard before.

As if on cue, a ranch Jeep raced toward her and screeched to a stop with a spray of gravel. Steele sprang from behind the wheel, but the man with him took his time getting out. He was a tad shorter and stockier than Steele, his hair a burnished chestnut rather than raven's-wing black, but side by side, there were more similarities than differences.

"Montana, meet my baby brother, Sloan."

"Our parents saved the best for last." Sloan removed his sunglasses to reveal dazzling blue eyes with faint lines at the corners. He seemed a more laid-back version of Steele, as if he had nothing but time and knew the rest of the world would wait for him. Or was that simply his facade? For she sensed he could, in his own way, be every bit as lethal as Steele.

His grip reminded her of Steele's, the intimacy with which he held her hand and sized her up at the same time. "I made the mistake of asking big brother here if he needed anything. Turned out he needed his plane. Not quite what I had in mind, but here I am."

"I'd do the same for you," Steele said.

"I'll remind you of those few well-chosen words."

Montana's gaze shifted from one brother to the other. "Why do I feel I've been left out of the loop?" She directed her words to Steele. "Are you going somewhere?"

"We," Steele said. "How soon can you pack an overnight bag?"

Montana turned to Sloan. "Can you excuse us for a moment, please?"

"Sure thing. I'll amble over to the bunkhouse and grab a coffee."

Montana turned on Steele. "What are you up to this time? And I'd appreciate the truth, if that's possible."

His eyes grew as steely as his name. "You need resort and

spa staff if you have a prayer of opening on time. You've been poring over that stack of résumés for days now."

"Which is no concern of yours," she said stiffly.

"Cut the bull. You know who I am. You know what I do."

"I know you lied."

His mouth tightened. "I do what has to be done. I don't always like it."

"I don't need your help."

"Montana, you're in over your head. You can't afford to delay the opening. I make the impossible happen."

Understatement! "Did I not make it abundantly clear last night that I'm not one to sit quietly and passively while you run the show?"

"Abundantly." His look rekindled the smoldering remnants of last night's adventure. She swore she could feel sparks dancing through her bloodstream as she glanced around to make sure no one could overhear.

"So this is how you retaliate? Wrest control back in whatever way you can?"

"If you have an issue about control, Montana, just come out and say it."

Her issue wasn't about control; that was Steele's thing. Hers was about need. And not turning into her mother.

"I'm trying to help you here, and you're too stubborn to recognize it."

"As long as helping me is also helping Steele Hardt."

"Damn right. You'd be stupid to refuse when I have the best interests of Black Creek front and center."

"Along with your own best interests."

"I haven't lost the golden touch yet."

"One day someone's going to take you down a peg."

"They're welcome to try."

Their eyes dueled as Montana pondered her options. Which did she fear more—fear of failure, or fear of needing someone? They were both huge.

She decided to address the one fear she could probably master. "I haven't been in a plane since Charlie . . . since Charlie's accident."

"Ever hear about getting back on the horse that threw you?"

"It's not the same."

"Of course not. But I promise you one thing: you'll forget you're even in the air, and that's a promise I look forward to keeping."

She was doing it again. Letting him distract her.

"I'm sure Helen has some happy pill I can take that will do the trick."

"Much better to put yourself in the hands of Steele. But it's your play all the way. Your deal. Your call."

"You're showing me your cards? That doesn't strike me as your way."

"I told you before, I do what has to be done. I know people in Vegas. In less than twenty-four hours, we can have the resort fully staffed, good to go."

It would be stupid to refuse. "You couldn't run this by me first?"

He lowered his voice to a throaty purr that sent tingles of memory dancing up and down her. "I had other things on my mind last night. I intended to talk to you this morning but you were sound asleep, and now Sloan's here."

"Damn it, Steele, you play fast and loose with the concept of teamwork."

"But I get results. Expecting someone?" A dust-covered van inched its way down the driveway.

"It must be that writer from *Spa* magazine, with her photographer. They're early."

"Put on your hostess smile. I'll go fire up the Hydrawalk."

"Thanks. And Steele, stay out of sight in case she recognizes you and gets the wrong idea."

"Gladly. It so happens I loathe reporters." He glanced at his watch. "We'll leave for Vegas right after lunch."

He disappeared before the van trundled to a stop and the driver's door opened to reveal a young woman with rainbow-tipped spiky white-blond hair. A slouchy young man in a surfing T-shirt with several cameras trailed behind her.

"Welcome to Black Creek," Montana said. "Any problems finding the place?"

"Not at all. I'm Zoe. This is Rob, *Spa* magazine's photographer."

"Good to meet you both," Montana said. "How do we get started?"

"Generally I like to start out just walking and chatting. Background stuff, like where you're from originally. Montana, perhaps?"

"Nothing so obvious. My family moved a lot, up and down the West Coast." As they spoke, the photographer prowled about snapping outdoor shots of the ranch.

"A nomadic background."

"You could say that."

"Our readers like the nontypical success story. Is Black Creek your first real home?"

Montana flashed to a memory of the Volkswagen van with surfboards strapped to the roof. "No, but I hope it's my last."

Zoe's colorful head danced this way and that, as if trying to take in everything at once. "The dude ranch has been here since the early 1900s, correct?"

"That's right. It was totally rustic and isolated in those early days. My late husband's father made a lot of improvements, work that was carried on by Charlie. The Oasis spa is over this way."

"Great. Hang on a second." She scribbled madly in a steno pad.

"Don't reporters use tape recorders?"

"It depends. Since I expect we'll be moving around a fair bit, I find this more convenient." She flipped a page. "How do you think your late husband would feel about the changes you're bringing about?"

Montana should have been prepared for all this probing into her background, but she wasn't. "Charlie was always forward-thinking," she said. "Resort guests will enjoy total luxury and pampering in the midst of a wilderness setting."

"Do you have a background in business?"

"No formal education."

"But you raised the money to do this privately."

"Obviously the people backing me believe in me, as well as Black Creek's future."

"What are your plans for the dude ranch?"

"That side of things remains virtually unchanged."

"Interesting to have two very different enterprises under one umbrella. Isn't that a difficult balance?"

Zoe didn't know the half of it, and Montana wasn't about to enlighten her. "I'm convinced the two venues will complement each other nicely."

Zoe consulted her notes. "Your late husband built the airstrip. Correct?"

Montana nodded. "Forward-thinking, like I said. One of the improvements I've implemented is to have it paved to accommodate larger aircraft. Did I mention Daniel Perri will be our executive chef?"

"Perri? That's a coup. Who have you hired as spa director?"

"I'm afraid I'm not at liberty to divulge their identity till the grand opening."

"Secrets at Black Creek?"

"Surprises," Montana corrected. "Wait till you see my pride and joy."

The Hydrawalk proved an enormous hit, and the remainder of the interview went smoothly. Still, Montana couldn't still her nagging suspicion that the journalist had been on a fishing expedition. She hoped she was wrong.

Because the interview ran long, she was left with mere minutes before she was scheduled to meet with Steele.

Helen watched her pack. "It's sweltering in the desert. Wear one of those darling sundresses of yours. And you must pack an evening dress, dear. One never knows."

"It's a business trip, Helen." Her words fell on deaf ears as Helen rummaged through her closet.

"This would be perfect."

Black, body-hugging, and stretchy, like an overgrown tube top with straps, the dress, Montana had to admit, would take her anywhere, plus it packed easily. She twisted it into a small knot and tossed it into her bag.

Helen smiled. "It never hurts a girl to combine a little pleasure along with the business. Vegas is such a fun city. Montana, I—" Helen was interrupted by the sound of a horn outside.

"That'll be Steele. What were you going to say?"

"Nothing that won't wait, dear. Have a nice time. And don't worry about the ranch while you're gone."

"I promise." She gave her mother-in-law a quick hug. "Behave while I'm away."

"Merciful heaven, I hope not."

Out front, Steele threw her bag in the back of the Jeep. She looked around. "Where's Sloan?"

"He's already at the plane. How did it go with the journalist?"

"Fine. How come I didn't know you own a plane?"

"There's a lot we still don't know about each other."

He slanted her a look that threatened to ferret out all her secrets without giving up any of his. She returned it in kind. Steele might be a gambler; Montana wasn't. Her secrets were all hers.

As the Jeep wheeled up to the freshly paved landing strip, Montana sat frozen in her seat. The sleek Falcon bore little resemblance to Charlie's light two-seater, but it was still much too small for her comfort level.

"All set?" Sloan ambled over to the Jeep and grabbed their bags.

She wanted to say no but clamped her lips shut. She'd forgotten all about checking Helen's pharmaceutical stash.

Steele looked over at her, hands clenched, white-knuckled in her lap. "You're going to be okay," he said.

"Easy for you to say." She took a breath and slid from the Jeep, feeling Steele's hand against the small of her back in silent support.

The stairway to the plane felt as wobbly as it looked, its movement keeping time with the butterflies in her stomach. Sloan was stowing their bags in a compartment at the front of the plane's cabin as Montana entered, ahead of Steele, what looked like a cozy den with deep leather club chairs, subdued lighting, and a plasma TV screen.

He made sure she was comfortably settled, then placed a glass of champagne in her ice-cold hand. She gave him a grateful half-smile and took a gulp.

"You're doing great," he said, buckling himself into the seat next to her.

"Nothing a little liquid courage won't put right." The plane's engine turned over and the shaky feeling in the pit of her stomach grew.

Steele reached over and took her free hand. "Sloan's a good pilot."

"So was Charlie."

She leaned back and closed her eyes as the plane taxied

down the newly paved runway. She didn't dare look out the window till they had lifted smoothly into the air.

"How long should it take us to get there?"

"A few hours, depending on the tailwind."

She nodded and turned to the window. Already they were above a layer of fluffy white clouds. Perhaps it was better she couldn't see land below; she could pretend they were in some sort of cotton cocoon.

Steele rose and closed the curtain between the cabin and the cockpit; then he touched a button and soothing jazz music wafted through the cabin. A second button lowered the window blinds as if by magic, and the lighting dimmed.

Montana felt some of her nervousness start to dissipate, then return with a vengeance when her seat started to recline beneath her.

"Relax," Steele said. "I want you to be comfortable." He pulled up a stool near her feet and tugged off her sandals. Taking her bare feet prisoner, he rubbed them between his large, sun-browned hands.

She flinched and tried to pull free. He flashed a teasing grin. "Don't tell me you're ticklish."

"I admit to nothing." But she jerked as he ran his thumbnail along the delicate arch.

"Like I said earlier, there's a lot we don't know about each other."

"Tell me one of your secrets."

"You might not believe this, but I know how to relax. And now I'm going to teach you." Slowly, gently, he began to massage her foot, starting with each individual toe. As his touch spread to probe the ball of her foot, then her heel, so did the pleasurable warmth that accompanied it. A sluggish heat, like barely warmed honey, preceded the pathway forged by his talented hands. Unlike his hands, the spill of warmth didn't stop at her ankle but continued up the length of her bare legs. She felt her muscles grow slack as her nerve endings sprang to life. Her skin prickled with awareness and the backs of her knees grew damp with perspiration, followed by a throb low in her belly.

She curled her toes into his hands with a blissful sigh as she floated in a relaxed place, eyes shut, focused solely on the magic of Steele's touch. At some point his mouth replaced his hands, licking her instep, then her toes, and desire chased through her bloodstream to burrow into her womanly nest of secrets.

"Maybe you do have access to my secrets," she murmured.

"I hope I know the important ones." His tongue followed the raging river of desire up the inside of her leg to her knee.

Limbs that felt too liquid and heavy to move burned with the need to have him touch her everywhere.

She unbuttoned the front of her flouncy red sundress and Steele gave a low growl of approval. "Have I told you I applaud your taste in undergarments?"

She smiled in satisfaction and smoothed her hands down her length, well aware the gossamer-sheer red demi bra and matching thong were more enticement to the male senses than wearing nothing at all.

"Oh, yeah." His hands cupped her breasts reverently, and

through the silk her nipples peaked to attention. He circled them with his thumbs while his fingertips molded and shaped her softness.

He leaned forward and lightly licked the silk-sheathed nipples. Montana moaned at the sensation of moist silk between her and the knowing tongue taking over the job started by his fingers.

She swiftly unbuttoned the front of his shirt, exploring the flex of muscles, the tightness of his belly, then ruffling the crisp matting of hair with her fingertips before she made the flat male nipples come to life.

She rubbed his belly with the back of her hand, her fingertips dipping teasingly just inside the waistband of his jeans.

"I love your hands on me," Steele said.

"I know what else you love."

As he traced the soft seam at the top of her legs, his fingertips so light against her skin they were barely more than a whisper, Montana undulated restlessly. Her silk thong rubbed against her, ineffectual stimulation when she burned for Steele's touch.

A touch he deliberately withheld, as he drew circles across her scantily covered Venus mound. "I love to make you come."

She slid the thong aside. "So what are you waiting for?"

"I'm seeing how long I can make you wait."

Montana knew she could easily turn the tables on him, but she elected not to. Let him do the work, since he was so set on having control.

She sat up and slid past him to help herself to more champagne.

She raised her glass his way. "You most effectively took my mind off being in the air."

The look on his face was priceless, and she bit back a triumphant smile.

One second he'd had her hot and panting beneath him, the next she was out of reach, and she knew he was wondering just how the control had slipped from him.

It was a simple equation, one she had no intention of sharing. As long as she didn't need him, he had no control over her. And she was determined to keep it that way.

"Nice try, Montana."

He came up behind her just as the plane hit a pocket of turbulence, jostling them into each other.

Montana shivered with excitement as he ran his hands across her bare skin, leaving a trail of fire in their wake. His belt buckle was cold against her belly but did little to cool the raging heat of her internal furnace. She felt him against her, lengthening and thickening through the coarse denim of his jeans as she wrapped her arms around his middle and rubbed against him, her breasts to his chest, her pelvis to his.

"You get off on making me wait."

He ripped off his shirt. "I get off on *you.* Period."

She took her time unfastening his belt and sliding down the zipper of his jeans, then smiled. "Show me."

Chapter Eleven

Steele slowly walked his fingers the length of her arms till their fingers linked. Then, his length flush against her, their eyes locked, he slowly guided her to the back of the plane.

Montana thrilled to the feel of him, his strength and mastery. She inhaled when he did, dragging air into her starving lungs; he took away her breath with just a look.

Her steps aligned with his in their heady dance of intimacy through the belly of the plane. Their journey ended at the upholstered built-in couch at the rear of the plane, where she landed on a pile of faux-fur throws with him atop her.

Impatiently she pushed at his jeans, tugged them down over his hips, then hooked them lower with her bare feet till he could kick them out of the way.

She felt his erection hard against her belly as he knelt above her, the proud and conquering male, secure in his power. He pushed her thong aside to test her heat and dampness with his fingers. She writhed up toward him, his fingers a tease, a promise of more. She whimpered in frustration, straining for more. Then he thrust into her.

Montana sighed in relief, rose up in welcome. The look of concentration on his face matched the intensity of each slow, sure stroke of possession as she clung to him and enjoyed the ride.

As she tightened her inner muscles around him, the pleasurable intensity deepened. She felt in every pore and nerve ending the way they matched each other's rhythm. Almost as if each knew the song the other sang in their heart.

How else would Steele know when to speed up and when to slow down, as he lifted her to the summit and held her there, hovered with her, not letting her go over?

She arched her hips to deepen the angle of penetration and gave a deep moan of pleasure at his response as she reached around to his backside, feeling the flex of his glute muscles as he moved inside her.

She loved the way he read her responses and matched them with his own. Shallow. Deep. Fast. Slow. The two of them blurred together into one kaleidoscope of sensation, whirling into orbit. An orbit Steele controlled.

The buildup resonated with raw power and Montana

hung there, suspended in everlasting pleasure, her senses strung so tight they almost hurt. Everything felt so damn good. Maybe she should always let Steele have his way.

She tightened her pelvic muscles and bore down, wondering if she could snap his control. He stopped moving to stare down at her, a knowing look of such intensity it seared into her soul. "Why did you stop?" she asked with mock innocence.

"You enjoy playing people, don't you?"

He had her there.

She zigzagged her nails across his back. "I enjoy you."

"You love to test their limits."

"Isn't that your special talent?"

"Careful, Montana. You might find out I play no limit."

Montana swallowed a bubble of fear. This man knew her, touched her in ways she'd never been touched. She couldn't let him close. Couldn't let him know his power.

"Sounds like fun." She matched her words to action, undulating her hips, muscles squeezing and releasing as she moved beneath him in a desperate frenzy. Anything to keep him from seeing too deep, reaching down inside her to touch her soul.

He smoothed back her hair, gave her another long, searching look she did her best to evade, then took over.

He raised her legs to rest on his shoulders, deepening the angle of his possession. His erection felt enormous inside her, deliciously huge. Was that him throbbing and pulsing with barely leashed passion? Or her?

Smooth as silk, in and out he thrust in perfect measured

rhythm and control, a control she longed to shatter. But once again he'd turned things around, giving himself full control. The angle, the speed, the pace.

All she could do was hang on and enjoy.

"Yes!" Her breath rose and fell in shallow pants as she clutched the faux fur, concentrating on one thing only: Steele. In her.

"Faster!"

He obliged, their joining a blur, and just when she thought she might expire from the intensity, he reached between them, found her swollen love knot, and sent her spinning out of control.

She held on, determined to take him with her. As internal pressure accelerated to the point where she shattered into a million splinters of ecstasy, she heard his hoarse cry as he spiraled into orbit alongside her.

Montana felt Steele's heart thud heavily against hers till she was no longer sure which heartbeat was his and which was hers. Two hearts that beat as one.

Lord help her! The fact that she longed to lie there and absorb the closeness of their coupling was the very reason she couldn't. She never allowed anyone this close.

Getting close led to loss. She couldn't bear more loss.

She scrambled to her feet, scooped up her discarded dress, and headed for the compact washroom.

In the dim light she peered closely in the mirror. Were those her eyes, so dark and troubled, above a mouth deep red and well kissed? Her hair was a tumbled mess and she braided it with hands that weren't quite steady.

Steele had gotten way too close for her peace of mind. Time to insert some distance between them.

She returned to the cabin. Steele must have felt the same, for he was nowhere to be seen. Feeling oddly deflated, she took a seat and pulled out her computer. She didn't look up when someone entered the cabin from the cockpit, pretending to be deeply engrossed in the jumble of letters on the screen.

Finally curiosity got the better of her, and she looked over to see Sloan next to her.

"Congratulations," he said.

"On what?" Montana asked.

"I've never seen my big brother quite so rattled."

"I doubt Steele gets rattled."

"Well, he's definitely off his game."

"You're jumping to conclusions if you think it has anything to do with me."

He sat back, that same unconscious pose of Hardt self-confidence. "Tell me about Black Creek."

She welcomed the distraction, warming to her subject as she told him about the ranch and its guests, the size and scope of the operation, her plans for the future as she tried to meld the old with the new in a complementary way.

So enthused was she, it was a long time before she realized Steele had joined them. She glanced from brother to brother. "Who's flying the plane?"

"A computer," Steele said. "I got lonely."

Sloan gave a lazy stretch. "Speaking of which, I'd better get back there." He rose to leave and Steele slid into his vacated seat.

"You're a pilot, as well?" she asked Steele.

"I don't like having to rely on others."

She knew that feeling well.

She leaned toward the window and pointed. "Is that where we're headed?" "That" being a huge glow of lights in the middle of nowhere.

"Sin City."

"It looks like enough megawatts burning to light up the entire country."

"Six thousand people a month are relocating there. A quarter century ago there were worries about a water shortage, but the Colorado River hasn't failed us yet."

"Like the Rogue River that feeds into Black Creek." She leaned forward for a better look, realizing just how small her world was.

This new world was overwhelming. Or was she overwhelmed by Steele? The feelings he stirred up in her exposed a raw nerve, exposed things she'd rather not look at. Not now, and not ever.

And yet he seemed to know how she was feeling. All those conflicting, churning emotions.

"It doesn't matter where I go, or how long I'm gone, it always gets to me when I come back. It's really something."

"It doesn't even look real."

"That's part of the appeal. A city where absolutely everything is larger than life, over the top."

The way he described his hometown, he could have been describing himself. "Would you be different if you'd grown up here?" she asked.

"Hard to say. Would you be different if your parents had stayed in one place?"

"I guess I'd be the same, only different."

"Exactly." The plane gave a little hiccup and her ears popped as they started to noticeably lose altitude. He reached over and caught her hand in his, holding it loosely as the plane descended and touched down on the tarmac, then taxied to a stop. "Welcome to Henderson Sky Harbor."

"This must be a busy airport."

"Not to mention the air force base in the northeast corner of the valley. Along with copious numbers of heliports."

"If you were talking in an effort to distract me, it worked."

He brushed a hand across her cheek. "I love to distract you."

Montana flinched and moved out of reach. Damn him! Couldn't he see the huge hands-off sign she worked so hard to erect? She stood and then felt silly, as there was no place to go till the door opened.

"I hate to tell you this, but if you're trying to get away from me, you're out of luck. You're stuck with me for a few days now."

"Exactly what you had in mind, I'm sure."

Luckily the door opened. Leaving Steele to deal with their bags, she headed for temporary freedom, only to recoil from the blast of hot, dry desert air.

"Don't worry, you'll acclimatize."

Montana doubted she'd ever acclimatize to Steele's way of doing things, as he whisked her into the divinely cool interior of a waiting limo.

"Help yourself to a beverage. I won't be long."

She leaned against the cool leather seat back and watched the Hardt brothers as they chatted with airport personnel whom they were obviously on friendly terms with.

Already Montana was afraid this was a bad idea. She had enough trouble with Steele on her own turf. Why place herself on the precarious slope of Steele's home ground?

He slid in next to her and eyed her critically. "You look tired."

"Thanks," she flipped. "That's a polite way of telling a woman she looks bad."

He reached for her. "You could never look bad."

She evaded his touch. "What's the plan?"

He opened a bottle of Corona and took a long drink, then offered her the bottle. She shook her head.

"I called ahead to a headhunter I use who really knows her stuff. She'll meet us at the hotel."

"Where I'm certain you booked us separate rooms."

"How about you relax and trust me?"

Trust. Such a simple little word, carrying such a huge load of emotional baggage. When had she stopped trusting the men in her life? When Duke died? When Charlie cheated on her the first time, or countless times thereafter? She didn't even trust Charlie's best friend, Melvin, yet he was the one who had made the resort possible by coming up with the investment capital she required.

"What about Sloan?" she asked, as the limo made its way from the airport into the flow of traffic.

"Why does it seem easier for you to trust my brother than to trust me?"

"What's your best guess?"

"Women do seem to favor Sloan's happy-go-lucky style."

"Over your dark, brooding intensity? What a surprise."

He leaned back and studied her. "Tell me about the man who died. And I don't mean your husband."

She blinked away an unexpected mistiness in her vision. "Duke was kind and gentle and generous, and asked for nothing in exchange."

"I'm guessing he was considerably older."

She nodded. "He was a guest speaker in my university business class. We hit it off; he became my mentor."

"And your lover."

"Not at first, but eventually." She sighed. "I never knew he was sick. I was devastated when he said good-bye. By the time I found out, it was too late. Like my father all over again."

"So how did you meet Charlie?"

"Duke had advised me on some good investments. I had enough money to quit my job and rent a beach house up north, in Cannon Beach. I was in an art gallery there, buying my first Lamotia piece. Charlie was there on vacation. We started to chat about art and life. I was intrigued by Black Creek, land that had been in the family for generations, a life that was stable and solidly rooted. Charlie didn't like to work and I did, so the marriage suited us both. I had a home and he had a ranch manager."

Outside, the streets were a barrage of signs and blinking lights and crowds and traffic. "Is it possible I'm claustrophobic already?"

Steele touched a button that opened the moon roof of the limo. "Does that help?"

She half smiled. "Not from the car, from the city. There's such a heady energy of noise and crowds and frantic busyness."

"That's normal for a lot of people."

"Thank goodness it's not normal for me. That's why a place like Black Creek is so important: people need the chance to recharge."

"Not everyone needs that."

"Do you?"

"I thrive in all environments."

He most certainly did. "The city that never sleeps. Are your parents still here?"

He nodded. "My mother owns a very successful lingerie shop. You should meet her; you two would get along famously."

Montana didn't know what to say. Here she was trying to distance herself from Steele and he was telling her she'd like his mother.

"And your father?"

"He runs a casino."

"What about your brother?"

"I'm sure we'll catch up with him later."

"I mean, what does he do?"

"He looks after the family ranch where we grew up."

"So the foreman stuff wasn't all fake."

"Nothing about me is fake."

He pointed out the sights. Caesars Palace. The Bellagio. The MGM Grand. Famous hotels and casinos that until now had only been names. There were so many lights, she swore she could hear an underlying hum of electricity, and the sidewalks were thronged with pedestrians of all ages.

"I didn't expect to see so many young children. I thought this was a playground for adults."

"Apparently a lot of those adults are parents who also like to gamble."

"Do you miss it?"

He leaned over and played with the tendrils of hair that had escaped her braid. "What's to miss? Everything in life is a gamble."

"I don't understand the gambler's psyche. Is it the thrill? The adrenaline rush?"

He shook his head. "For the pro, it's all about being smarter than everyone else."

His words gave her pause. Hmm, she might just take that as a challenge.

The limo pulled up in front of the Black Opal, where they were whisked to the penthouse by way of a glass-walled private elevator on the outside of the building.

"Now I'm really overwhelmed."

"Don't be. It simply made sense when we were renovating. You wouldn't think it's hard to be anonymous in a town like Las Vegas, but it can be. I remember times it took hours just to get through the lobby and the casino to the elevators. This way I'm visible only when I choose to be."

The elevator doors slid open soundlessly to reveal a marble-floored salon decorated in various shades of white, a cool contrast to the desert heat. Montana found it beautiful, and as sterile as a dentist's waiting room. All that saved it was the view. Las Vegas, the jewel in the desert, sprawled in every direction, three hundred and sixty degrees.

As Montana took it all in, a petite blonde, nearly invisible on the lily-white couch, rose and greeted Steele with an enthusiastic kiss. "You haven't changed the elevator code, you bad boy."

"Kyra." Steele returned her greeting with an enthusiastic hug of his own. "I didn't expect you till tomorrow. This is Montana Blackstone."

The blonde kept one arm possessively looped around Steele's waist. "Now, why wasn't I told Montana Blackstone is a beautiful woman?"

Montana recognized the possessive gleam in the other woman's eye as she stepped forward and offered her hand. "Thank you so much for your help. Steele assures me you're the best."

"Does he, now?" Kyra released Steele with seeming reluctance. "As usual, he continues to challenge me."

There was no mistaking the double meaning in the other woman's words and Montana felt a sudden, unwelcome flare of jealousy.

She'd been hurt by Charlie's philandering, but had never been jealous.

Montana flashed them both a brilliant smile. "Will you two please excuse me while I freshen up?" She turned to Steele. "Which way?"

He led her through a bedroom finished in sumptuous jewel tones, fit for a sultan, into a bathroom straight out of *Lifestyles of the Rich and Famous.* Marble and glass galore surrounded a party-sized raised tub overlooking the city.

"Your designer must have a hedonistic streak."

Steele shrugged. "It's all part of the package."

The Vegas package? she wondered. Or the Steele Hardt package?

"It's a far cry from the bunkhouse at Black Creek."

"I'm adaptable."

So am I, Montana reminded herself as she splashed cool water on her face and dug through her purse for a comb. This time her hair defied all attempts to tame it into a braid, so she allowed it to settle into shoulder-length waves. Her wrinkled dress was beyond smoothing—akin to the way she felt, manhandled by Steele.

She gave herself a long, bolstering look in the mirror. *Showtime.*

The sun had dipped low, bathing the penthouse in mysterious mauve twilight, while the sky was streaked with vivid pink slashes of color, nature's last hurrah for the day.

Steele had turned on a few low lights in the salon and the soft sounds of muted jazz curled from hidden speakers. A bottle of Veuve chilled in the ice bucket next to two waiting flutes.

Steele stood at the window with his back toward her, looking comfortably relaxed. Silent as she was in bare feet, he turned toward her. He must have seen her reflection in the window. She glanced around. "No Kyra?"

"We'll meet with her tomorrow, as planned."

She walked over and picked up a glass of champagne. "I bet that went over like lead."

"What do you mean?"

"Steele, the woman all but hung a 'private property' sign around your neck."

"Kyra and I are simply old friends."

Perhaps in *his* mind! She was saved from further comment by the chime of the elevator, heralding the arrival of a uniformed waiter pushing a covered serving table.

"Evening, Mr. Hardt. The dining room?"

"The coffee table is fine, James. We'll keep it informal."

"What's this?" Montana asked.

"I thought we'd eat in, if that's agreeable with you."

"Whatever you like." She moved to the open French doors and stepped onto the balcony. The outside temperature was like a comfortable warm caress on her skin, and a traffic hum rose from the street below. Behind her, she could hear the muted clink of dishes and cutlery. In the distance, she could see the Eiffel Tower, the roller coaster of New York–New York, and the MGM Grand. Searchlights swept the sky farther off, while the hyper energy nearby seemed to envelop her. She took a long, calming breath, trying to dispel it.

She could do this. She could keep Steele at arm's length,

dodge killer looks from his old girlfriend, and hire the right people to work at Black Creek.

Behind her she sensed Steele's presence, then felt his hands on her hips and his lips brushing the nape of her neck.

"Dinner is served."

Chapter Twelve

Montana spun about to face him.

"Do you go the extra mile for all your clients?"

"You're not technically a client."

"What am I, then?"

His smile was wry. "A challenge."

"And you like to be challenged."

"You're discovering all my secrets."

She laughed. "Now, that I refuse to believe." She waved a hand to encompass the city spread at their feet. "Hard to believe this is your home."

"Home is any place I happen to be."

She searched his face. "You never put down roots?"

"I never stay long in one game."

For Steele, everything was a game. And two could play.

She took hold of his shirt front and drew closer. "Should I thank Helen for her meddling?"

"She meant well." When she swayed closer, he stepped back. "Come in and eat."

Strangely deflated, she followed him inside to where a myriad of scents teased her senses. Duck confit, lemongrass chicken, and ginger prawns on saffron rice—further reminders that they were a long way from Black Creek.

"I guess you found the bunkhouse fare pretty plain."

He set the silver serving spoon down with a very deliberate clatter. "Why do you insist on doing that?"

"Doing what?"

"Marking the contrast between here and the ranch."

"You can't deny the difference."

"Right here, right now is where we are. Together. Once we accomplish what we came for, we'll head back."

The "we" word: one more thing she didn't trust. Montana gave a jerky nod, aware she hadn't exactly been a gracious guest. "Thank you for realizing I was too tired to go out to eat."

"I notice everything about you."

She swallowed and reached for her champagne glass. He was doing it again. Getting into her space, seeing too much.

His hand atop hers stopped her midmovement. "I know I'm making you uncomfortable. I'm doing it deliberately. It's good to be jolted from our comfort zones."

She tugged her hand free. "Do you profess to always know what's best?"

"I try. Relax and enjoy the meal before I show you around the casino. We'll find out if you have gambling in your blood."

How could she relax when the man across from her was a constant challenge? Montana took a breath, kicked off her shoes, and pulled up one of the oversized cushions near the coffee table as Steele filled their plates.

"You have an impressive art collection."

"I like to support new talent."

"From an investment point?"

"I buy on instinct. Artists who aren't afraid to express their passion. Like you, with your pieces by Lamotia."

He'd seen through her, the fact that she attempted to buy or borrow passion from those who embodied it. To vicariously experience the raw passion of others, having learned to keep her own well hidden.

Silence stretched between them, heightening Montana's discomfort. This was all a terrible mistake. She ought never to have agreed to this junket. But she wanted to make Black Creek the best of the best so, uncomfortable as it was to accept help, she needed Steele.

"You have a superb chef," she said.

"Don't get any ideas about stealing her. My people are loyal." He refilled her champagne flute. "What was your life like when you were dancing?"

"It was a challenge at the time, a means to an end, but never a passion."

"Was Duke in your life then?"

She nodded. "He knew my goal was financial independence, and dancing was the means to that end."

"And now Black Creek inspires your passion?"

"Taking it to the next level does."

"And then what?"

She had no answer, having never looked beyond the present. Life was safer that way, less prone to disappointment.

She was relieved when he changed the subject. "I see that Chef sent up chocolate fondue for dessert."

"Naughty Chef. What is she thinking?"

"That I'm entertaining a beautiful woman, and she's determined I do it in style." He unveiled the chocolate fondue with a flourish, dipped his finger in, and licked it clean, watching her watching him.

Did she see an invitation in that dark, deep gaze? Or a challenge?

Montana jumped to her feet. This was getting way out of hand. Steele was calling all the shots: the plane, the car, the meal, and now her entire staff. When had control slipped so insidiously from her hands?

"Where are you going?"

"I'm having a shower."

In the luxurious bathroom, she stripped and stepped beneath the sharp spray of water coming at her from a half dozen directions. It would take far more than a simple shower to wash Steele from her mind and her life.

Was this her pattern? From a strong man like Duke, her early mentor who had seen into her starved inner soul, to a weak man like Charlie who barely knew her and didn't care, back to a strong man like Steele, who knew her inside out?

"He's just a means to an end," she said.

Steele stared at the back of the bathroom door, which Montana had closed with more force than necessary. He was going out of his way to make her uncomfortable and doing a damn fine job of it. Anything to bluff the other player. Truth be told, Montana was unsettling him without even trying. Fortunately, she had no idea.

He heard water running and knew she was in there all warm and wet and soft and smooth. If you didn't count her prickles, that is. She morphed into porcupine quills from time to time to protect her soft vulnerabilities.

He was deep in the throes of enjoying his image of Montana, hair wet and streaming over her milky, perfect breasts, when he heard the elevator arrive. When the doors slid open his mother stepped out, followed by his father. He hid his surprise at the sight of the two of them together.

His mother was as beautiful as ever; people constantly mistook her for his sister. She kept herself in good shape, and if she had a little help from time to time, it was none of his business.

"Steele. I've missed you." She stepped forward and hugged him warmly. He hugged her back, then turned to his father. Tanned and tuxedoed, with a thick head of silver hair, Rake still turned heads when he walked through the casino.

"Good to have you back, son."

"It's only temporary," Steele said quickly.

He caught the look the two of them exchanged and suddenly he was four years old again, feeling very responsible for his year-younger brother as his parents broke the news that they were getting divorced and sending the boys to live with their grandfather.

"We have exciting news," his mother said. "And we're so glad you're here so we can tell you in person."

"Anyone besides me want a drink?"

"Sure." His father strolled through the living room, oblivious, but his mother noticed the two champagne glasses and the warm chocolate fondue.

"You're entertaining. We've come at a bad time."

Steele shrugged. "You're here now. May as well give me the news." He poured single-malt Scotch for his father, white wine for his mother.

His mother looked at his father, who nodded. She beamed. "We're getting married."

"Who to?" Steele asked mildly.

"To each other, silly." She giggled. "And we're going around the world on our honeymoon."

"Which is why we're glad you're back to run the casino," his father said.

"This seems rather sudden," Steele said when some comment seemed required.

"This time, we figure we're mature enough to know our own minds," Rake said.

"Your father swept me right off my feet."

"What? Again?" Steele asked cynically.

His mother flashed him a reproachful look, designed to make him feel guilty.

It worked, the way it always did, and he crossed the room to reassure her. "I'm not warped and cynical because of your divorce."

"No," she said. "You and your brother both are. I only hope that one day you'll be able to fall in love."

"Stranger things have been known to happen."

As if on cue, he heard the door open behind him, and spun around. Damn! Montana had heard that last exchange. He could tell by the hesitant look on her face and her stride. She'd changed into a short, stretchy black dress that fit her like skin and showed off every sinuous movement.

"You didn't tell me to expect company."

"People love to keep surprising me. Montana Blackstone, meet my parents. Angel and Rake."

"A pleasure." She extended her hand to Angel first. "Steele told me you have an amazing lingerie store I must check out while I'm here."

Angel's smile widened, slid from Montana to Steele and back to Montana. "Steele said that?"

Steele inwardly groaned, knowing full well how his mother would misinterpret such a random remark.

"Indeed. A woman can't have too much lingerie." Montana turned her attention to Rake. "Wouldn't you agree?"

"No arguments there." His father's famous blue eyes twinkled. He was eating this up.

"Steele had just promised to show me around the casino," Montana continued. "Perhaps we can all go."

"A fabulous idea," Angel said, linking her arm through Montana's. "How do you feel about weddings?"

"That all depends on who is getting married. And why."

"Exactly: the unending passion of love. I'm afraid Steele is a bit cynical."

"Mother." His voice was low and threatening.

"Can I help it if I long for my boys to be as happy as I am?"

"What mother wouldn't?" Montana said innocently as Steele left to get changed.

Steele's mother would never know just how grateful Montana was for her presence as the four of them toured the casino on the first floor of the hotel. It was slow going, with customers continually stopping one or both of the Hardt men. They were high rollers, Angel confided; their presence was integral to the success of any casino. Montana found the lights and noise overwhelming as they made their way through a maze of bars, gaming tables, and slot machines over to the poker room. Left on her own, she was certain she would need a trail of bread crumbs to find her way back.

"Do you gamble?" Angel asked.

Montana shook her head. "I feel like a deer caught in the headlights," she confessed. "I don't know where to look first."

"If you live here long enough, I think you get immune to

it." She turned Montana in the direction of Steele and Rake. "Would you look at those two." She shook her head. "Rake's name is a holdover from his gambling days, when they called him Rake-It-In. He never lost, or so he claimed, and the nickname stuck. Unfortunately things came too easily to him, and he took everything for granted."

"Including you?" Montana said.

"I wouldn't accept it. That's why I left." She sighed. "But I never stopped loving him. And now he has a new appreciation for who I am."

"I'm glad."

Angel's happy glow was contagious. "I wanted my boys to be strong and independent, but I fear I may have made them too much so."

"Steele certainly lives up to his name."

"They both do."

As the men reached their side, Montana was struck by this new side to Steele, as if he'd changed his persona along with his clothes. Gone was the denim-clad ranch foreman; in his place was a dark-suited, successful casino owner. How many more personalities did he have?

"I'm always worried when we leave the girls alone for a few minutes," Rake said, putting his arm around Angel's waist. "Never know what they might take it into their heads to say about us."

"Don't flatter yourself," Angel said. "We have far more interesting things to talk about. Like shoes. Can we leave now?"

"I wanted to show Steele how the work on the Opus Lounge is coming along."

"Steele doesn't need a tour; he knows the way."

"I intended to check it out while I'm here," Steele said. "When's it scheduled to open?"

"Three weeks. Which you'd know if you ever spent any time here these days."

"I don't need to," Steele said easily. "I have you."

"Time was when you lived, breathed, and slept the Black Opal," Rake said.

Angel dug a not very delicate elbow into his side. "Unlike you, Steele has broader interests."

Rake shot Steele and Montana a mock salute. "I've got my orders. Go check out the lounge, you two. How long are you in town?"

"A day or two at most," Steele said. "Montana has to get back."

Angel and Rake exchanged a weighted glance that made Montana shift uncomfortably. Steele seemed to sense it, for he stroked her bare arm, offering silent support.

"We'll go have a quick look at the Opus." He gave his mother a quick hug. "And I'll catch up with you both before we leave."

There it was again. That "we" word that Steele threw around so casually.

They were on their way to the elevator when Steele stopped suddenly near one of the roulette tables. Instantly, Montana saw why. Standing near the dealer, looking smug, was Murdoch, and judging from the pile of chips in front of him he was on a winning streak. Steele caught Montana's hand in his and made his way to the other man's side.

"Having a good night, I see," he said casually.

"You know what they say: win some, lose some. I see you've got your spoils." He looked past Steele to Montana with an open leer and suddenly she wished she was showing less skin. "Apparently you *can* take the girl off the ranch and the ranch out of the girl."

"Glad to see you're not a poor loser, Murdoch."

"Are you kidding? If you came to bring me luck, I clearly don't need it."

"Well, given what you've lost here over the years, I can afford your winning streak tonight."

Montana hadn't noticed Steele's signal, but suddenly a waitress placed a snifter of cognac in front of Murdoch.

"A special vintage for special guests," Steele said. "Have a good night."

"I shouldn't have brought him out to the ranch, should I?" Montana said as they reached the bank of elevators. "I didn't realize what he was like."

"Better to humor him," Steele said. "Did you invite him to the grand opening?"

"Yes. Was that a mistake?"

"Nah, he's harmless. And not nearly as powerful as he thinks he is."

Steele used a special key card for their next ride in the elevator.

"What's the Opus Lounge we're supposed to check out?"

"A concept Rake dreamed up. An entire floor designed to accommodate 'members only.'"

After the noise and lights of the casino, the Opus was a

welcome retreat. Subdued lighting, thick carpet, and understated elegance was everywhere she looked. A curving bar followed the contours of the room to the seclusion of built-in banquettes, which afforded optimal privacy while still providing a view of the center stage dance floor.

"It'll operate like the old-world gentlemen's clubs." Before she could open her mouth, he added, "Don't worry. Women will be able to join, as well. Members can come anytime for a quiet drink and read the paper, entertain a client, or join in their favorite game of chance."

She ran her hand along the sleek leather of a high-backed chair near the fireplace. "What inspired this?"

"It was Rake's idea. He wanted to create the type of place he would have frequented back in his glory days."

"Back when life was slower and the world seemed a little less small."

"Exactly."

"I like it," Montana said. "It embodies what I'm trying to do with the resort, giving people a break from the hurly-burly."

"A home away from home," Steele said. "Rake's smart and he's usually never wrong."

Montana made her way onto the discreetly lit dance floor in the center of the room. "You'll use this for shows or dances, or what?"

"Anything," Steele said. "Watch this."

He touched a button and the floor beneath her lit up even more and rose about a foot, forming a stage. He touched another button and a shiny metal dance pole rose out of the floor, illuminated by a single spotlight. Music spilled provocatively from hidden speakers, a song she knew well.

"Sorry," Steele said. "I'll turn it off."

"No, leave it," Montana said. Slowly, as if in a dream, she saw herself reach out and take hold of the pole.

Chapter Thirteen

When the cold metal bit her palm, her fingers curled around it automatically. Her audience was out there watching from the shadows, faceless. Unable to see them, she retained anonymity.

A well-remembered rush of power surged through her blood. Out there lurked the watchers, where they could see but not touch. Anonymous, out of reach, she did as she pleased, touched and moved at will, all the while remaining safe.

She kicked off her shoes and her feet found their way

through the familiar music—as if it had been hours rather than years. Clearly, the body never forgot.

She twirled around the pole, then lifted one leg and elegantly wrapped it around the pole as she spun on the opposite foot. Her movements never faltered. The music swirled through her, transported her back to her former life. Grasping the pole with both hands, she did a full spin, both feet off the ground, feeling a familiar rush of exhilaration as the room sped past in a blur.

She had control, the safe and necessary space between herself and her audience. Feet on the ground, she finished the spin, rose up on her tiptoes, released one hand and raised the other up high, her back arched, her hair brushing the ground. Pulling herself up, she spun under her arm and recovered, spine against the pole. She let go and crossed her arms over her chest, played with the straps of her dress, sliding them up and down her bare arms.

Next she dragged her fingertips across her breasts and up over her shoulders, where, arms overhead, she took firm hold of the pole, twirled, arched her back, then rotated her hips in slow, seductive circles.

With one arm snaked around the pole she spun full front; then, with a seductive shrug of her shoulders, she wriggled her arms free from the straps of her dress.

Suddenly her solitude was shattered. Steele appeared with her on stage, illuminated from below, his face in shadow.

That wasn't the way it was supposed to happen!

She was safe up here. Out of reach. Powerful and in control.

Or not.

Her safe distance evaporated. The cold metal pole against her back blocked escape as Steele brought his body flush against hers. The music receded into the background.

"It won't work, Montana."

She licked her lips. Now the spotlight caught him as well as her.

She strove to keep things light. "I'm a little out of practice. Was I that bad?"

He plunged his hands through her hair, raking her scalp. "You were magnificent. Sexy and strong. But for every wall you try to throw up between us, expect me to tear it down with my bare hands. Don't think I don't know what you were doing up here. I know you. I see into your soul. I recognize you the way I recognize myself."

How dare he violate her safe space and presume so freely. Invade her soul, along with her body. She raised one arm and swung at him. He caught her arm easily in midair, blocking the blow. She raised her free hand and made a fist, which he caught as well, his fingers manacling her wrist.

She glared at him.

He glared back.

The stage, the music, the man before her. All was a blur just before they came together, heat and passion fused in a kiss. A meeting of mouths and minds and consequences be damned. She was full of him, surrounded by him, consumed by him.

He peeled down the front of her dress and feasted on her breasts. She clutched his head, her fingers tangled in his hair.

Heat and light and music, the present and the past, throbbed through her in a kaleidoscope of raw emotion.

She rejected the emotion and concentrated on the physical. The coldness of the lit stage beneath her bare feet. The solid support of the pole behind her. The soft fullness of Steele's hair. The way the heat of his mouth invaded her bloodstream and flowed into her limbs.

She widened her stance for balance as Steele's hungry mouth reclaimed hers. His chest crushed her bare breasts, the fabric of his jacket a new and different stimulant after the seeking heat of his lips and tongue. She rubbed against him. He rubbed back, his hips hard against her pelvis. Her hands burrowed beneath his shirt, seeking his skin as she clutched his hips and urged him closer.

She could feel the way he grew hard against her, and rolled her hips across his distended length. His nails raked her thighs as he pulled the hem of her dress slowly up her legs.

She moaned into him as he pressed his erection against her heated portal. She pivoted her hips back and forth in a suggestive move, seeking increased pressure, needing release.

His breathing was as ragged as her own. She unbuttoned his shirt and sighed softly as his chest kissed her breasts. The crisp texture of his chest hair further teased her sensitive nipples, sending a zing of electricity down to where his fingers probed, seeking her pleasure pearl, inflaming her even more.

"Hang on to me."

She did as she was told, digging her fingers into his shoulders. With one hand he clutched the pole above her head, supporting them both, as his other hand teased her hidden jewel. At the same time his hips danced against hers in slow seductive time to the music, against the pole.

It was too much. Too intense. The past seeped into the present, leaving her exposed and totally vulnerable.

"Stop fighting me." His breath was a warm seduction in her ear. "Let go."

How could she possibly let go? He was ripping away every last vestige of her protective outer shell, forcing full exposure of the here and now.

When she finally let go, a release of the body and the mind, her scream of pleasure echoed through the empty room and vibrated through both her and Steele.

Before she knew what had happened, Steele swept her into his arms and carried her off the stage to the velvet banquette. He lay her down carefully, as if aware just how fragile she was.

"Much better." He unfastened his pants and his cock sprang gloriously free. Before she even had time to admire his primal male beauty, he buried himself inside her.

She held him tight, hung on for the ride, aware that everything between them was different now. They were lost, yet they were found. An intense awareness of themselves and each other that heightened the experience, as two became one.

Pleasure reverberated through her as his cock filled and refilled her in such a way that she would never be empty again. As he lifted her to pinnacles of new pleasure and she shattered into prisms of light and mystery, she tightened her hold on him, inside and out, determined to take him with her.

Her body undulated beneath his in a rocket dance of pleasure upon pleasure, each sending the other to a new fever pitch of ecstasy.

As she spiraled away in one last free fall, she heard his hoarse cry of satisfaction, as he, too, tumbled over the edge of beyond.

Later, as they straightened their clothing and made their way back up to the penthouse, Steele mentally congratulated himself on exposing the real Montana. There were no more walls or poses or prickles. Just soft, vulnerable woman.

But as she curled up trustingly against him in bed later, he couldn't sleep for one troubling thought. What the hell had he done?

Steele stirred, reluctant to rip himself from the best dream of his life, centered around the divine sensation of something warm and wet near his groin.

He squeezed his eyes shut and willed the feeling to continue. When it did, his eyes flew open to focus on a divinely naked Montana kneeling next to him, holding the dish of chocolate fondue.

"It seemed a shame to waste something this yummy." She licked her chocolate-coated finger, dipped it in the bowl, then held it out for him to take a taste.

He pulled her over onto him, then dabbed some chocolate on her breast.

She laughed and rolled next to him. He swooped over and

licked the chocolate from her nipple, feeling it harden beneath his tongue, in direct contrast with the way she softened in his arms.

This was a new Montana. Soft. Playful. No thorns. No barriers for him to tear down. He rolled on top of her, wondering for a second if perhaps he'd left her too exposed.

She nipped at his chin, leaving a smear of chocolate. Beneath him, her body was as liquid and melting as the chocolate fondue.

"Aren't you forgetting a key component?"

"What's that?"

"The fruit."

"You mean this?" She reached past him to the fruit bowl on his side table.

"Exactly." He plucked a strawberry, bit into it, then used the juice to rouge her nipples. "What's chocolate without strawberries?"

"Or bananas?" She had one in her hand that she brandished through the air like a toy sword before he wrestled it away.

Triumphantly he half unpeeled it, dipped the exposed end in the fondue, and drew a chocolate line down her body from her breasts to her navel, then over her Venus mound to nuzzle that most responsive part of her.

She squirmed encouragingly beneath him, her eyes widening as he first rubbed insinuatingly, then inserted the banana's tip inside her.

In and out went their game, the fruit softening along with Montana as he used it to stimulate her. She got right into the game, flexing her hips in time to his rhythm, her breathing increasing along with the pace. At the crucial moment, he shot the banana out of its skin up inside of her.

"Steele!"

"It's okay, I've got it."

Pushing her legs apart, he proceeded to nibble the banana out of her, making sure he enjoyed her ripeness along with the fruit.

He'd never felt her so hot, so crazy and creamy, so frantically on the edge of release, and he took his time, savoring her taste along with the smell and feel of her aroused state, until finally he had licked her clean.

"What a great idea for breakfast." He slid her length, licking sweet dessert from sweet woman. Along her rib cage to the concave of her stomach, then lower, he delighted at the way she opened herself to him.

"I bet you never knew you were ticklish, did you?"

"There's a lot I didn't know about myself," she said, her tone suddenly far too serious. "I didn't know how much I like to play."

"You can't work all the time." He ran his tongue along the soft skin of her inner thigh and outlined the crease at the juncture while she shivered with anticipation.

He spread open her lips and admired the moist, beckoning pinkness of her quivering inner beauty. "Hold this for me," he said, replacing his hands with her own just before he dipped in for another taste.

"Aren't you full yet?"

"Of you? Never."

She obliged, exposing her moist inner secrets for his sampling pleasure. She was hot, sweeter than the chocolate-banana aperitif. Moans of pleasure escaped her throat as she rolled her head from side to side on the pillow. Her inner lips blushed; the shell-like shape enticed him near, begged for his kiss. In its tiny hood, her clitoris quivered and pulsed as he outlined it with his tongue. When he sucked it gently, she reared up and bucked beneath him, an intense release rocking her from head to toe.

He absorbed the aftershocks that continued to rack her body and felt the power of her sex meld with his, rendering him powerful and omnipotent. Not just his cock, his entire body was on fire for her.

She reached for him, her hand coated in chocolate, her touch slippery and erotic at the same time.

"Yummy." She feasted on him like a starving woman, her pumping hand and ravenous mouth working in tandem till he stopped her.

"I'm not done with you yet," she said. Her loose hair brushed his thighs teasingly, further inflaming his out-of-control senses.

"Nor I with you."

He lifted her up and onto nature's joystick. She paused and rubbed the head against herself, circling her lips, brushing her clit. The pulsing rush of blood to his cock made him light-headed.

He pushed up into her just as she slid down onto him. The friction was divine and he lost himself in the pleasure of her possession as she rode him into forever. Up and down, back and forth, pivoting in circles, she used him as shamelessly as he used her. Her breasts bobbed within reach and he palmed them, loving the way they leapt for him, adoring his touch. She purred low in her throat and rearranged herself so that he hit her G-spot; then she exploded into an array of fireworks that carried him right along with her.

He hadn't even started to recover when she was up pouring water and bath bubbles into the tub, urging him to join her. The crazy woman refused to sit still.

"Don't you ever need to recover?"

"I told you, sex energizes me. We have a lot to do today. But if you're a good boy and climb into the tub, I might bring you a glass of champagne."

She must be part vampire, draining his vital body fluids every time they had sex, to replenish herself and leave him totally depleted.

But the sight of her coming toward him carrying two glasses of champagne, glowing in the aftermath of their sexual romp, stirred him in unexpected ways and fired up a possessive streak he hadn't been aware of. *His woman.* And he'd kill any other man who had the pleasure of being responsible for that after-sex vigor.

She set the champagne down and climbed into the tub, where he lolled, his head on the rim, eyes half shut, watching her. "Why so serious?" she asked.

"I'm thinking. Do you want me to sit in on the interviews?"

"Kyra's done the preliminaries, correct?"

He nodded.

"And you trust her?"

"She's never let me down."

"Let's do an interview panel with the three of us, then. You'll read her well enough to know her picks."

"Whatever you would like." He started to get up.

"Where are you going?"

"Calling my staff to set up an interview room downstairs for us."

"Can you order me some breakfast, please? I'm starving."

Montana picked up a bright yellow rubber duck toy on the side of the tub. Why had she never realized playing could be so much fun? "Hurry back," she said, scooping a handful of bubbles and blowing them in his direction.

She was bobbing the duck through the suds this way and that when it suddenly started to vibrate in her hand. She slid low in the tub, laughing. Trust Steele to have every type of toy.

She timed his return so he'd find her perched on the edge of the tub, running the vibrating toy over her shoulders and arms, then to her breasts. He stopped short, paused, then advanced more slowly.

"You took so long, I had to start without you," she said in her sexiest tone.

He stood at the side of the tub looking so shell-shocked, she almost felt sorry for him. Gracefully she slid her legs apart and swam the duck up and down her stomach to her inner thighs. The towel around his waist formed an interesting tent, proving he wasn't quite as spent as he thought.

She stood and made her way across the huge tub. "Are you coming in?"

He dropped the towel.

"I could come to you," she purred.

"No need." He stepped into the tub and reached for the toy.

"Mine," Montana said.

"For now." His eyes never left hers as he sat back down and reached for his champagne.

She was playing to an audience of one now. No barriers. No anonymity. Just Steele.

As he stretched out in the tub and made himself comfortable, she stood directly over him, one leg on either side of him. This man who knew all of her secrets had taken the time to teach her how to play.

She let her hips sway from side to side, aware of his hungry gaze as she guided the toy up and down her midsection, each descent getting closer and closer to her inner sanctum.

The toy's vibration seemed to reverberate straight through to her spine, a pleasant, churning stimulation, heightened by Steele's bold gaze.

"Pleasure yourself," he said.

"Everything I do brings me pleasure."

She bent over and shared the toy's rhythm, fisting it the length of Steele's eager erection. He reached up and gifted her breasts with his special touch, a touch that burned its way to her womb.

She knelt to straddle him as the toy swam between her

sex and his. Back and forth the two of them rocked, first together, then apart, then back together.

As another orgasm undulated through her and Montana careened backward, Steele reached out and caught her, letting himself go at the same time in a fountain of churning bubbles and frothy ejaculate.

Nestled against him, Montana felt secure for the first time ever, feeling he would always be there to catch her.

As usual, Kyra didn't let him down. All the candidates for the interviews were professional and highly qualified.

Because he'd built his success on his ability to watch, then turn his observations into well-timed responses, he barely said a word as the two women lobbed the interview ball back and forth like well-matched tennis players.

All of which left him feeling pretty darn redundant at the end as Montana and Kyra compared shortlists, discussed the merits of various candidates, and made final decisions, with Kyra promising to contact the successful applicants.

"Thank you for everything you did to help me create my dream team," Montana said.

"Hey, when you have a dream . . ." Kyra left the rest unfinished, as if her meaning was obvious. Which it was, to Montana. How did women do that? More than merely creating a bond, they seemed to "get" each other.

"It's been a pleasure working with you," Montana said sincerely.

"Likewise," Kyra said as the two women packed up their briefcases.

"You must come out to Black Creek for a getaway, as my guest."

"I'd love that," Kyra said.

"Steele would fly you out, wouldn't you, Steele?" She gave his arm an encouraging pat, like he was some sort of family pet.

"Anytime," Steele said, unable to put his finger on what was bothering him. He should be happy Montana and Kyra hit it off so well, not feel like a third wheel.

Was it the way Montana seemed to take for granted that he'd be around and accessible? Or the way it felt so natural for her to touch him, when he doubted she even realized she was doing it?

Kyra pecked him on the cheek. "I have to get back to the office," she said, turning to Montana, and the two women hugged for what seemed a long time.

"See you later for drinks?" Kyra said.

"Whenever you can get away. Just give me a call on my cell." The door closed silently behind Kyra.

"You two are having drinks later?" Steele definitely didn't like the third-wheel twinge he felt.

"You're welcome to join us," Montana said.

"I'll probably be busy." Damn, he sounded like a petulant child.

"That's what we thought."

He was just about to suggest he and Montana grab a late lunch when his mother breezed into the boardroom.

"There you are. It took me forever to track you down."

Before he could open his mouth, Montana spoke up.

"Sorry, I had my phone turned off during the interviews."

Steele didn't hide his surprise. "You weren't looking for *me*?" he said to his mother.

Angel shook her head. "Montana and I have a date to go wedding-dress shopping."

"How long will you be?"

"Who knows?" Angel said breezily. "Surely you can amuse yourself for a few hours with your father and your brother."

Montana shoved her briefcase into his hand. "Be a doll and drop this upstairs for me, okay?" She pecked his cheek, not unlike Kyra, his mother gave him a quick hug, and he was left alone trying to figure out just what had happened and why it was bothering him so much.

"This will be such fun," Angel said. "I never had a daughter to go shopping with. Are you and your mother close?"

"No," Montana said, realizing it had been far too long since she had spoken to her mother.

"That's too bad," Angel said.

"I don't even know why," Montana said. "All I know is I didn't want to turn out like her. She always seemed like a shadow—first of my father, then, after he died, of her second husband."

"So you've taken the opposite swing of the pendulum and become totally independent?"

"I wanted to make sure I never needed anyone."

"Montana," Angel said softly. "We all need people in our lives. That's not a weakness. The right people are a gift."

"How do you know who's a good fit?"

"Instinct, I suppose, coupled with experience. But I do know that if you continually expect people to let you down, they'll do exactly that."

Montana fell silent, studying the racks of wedding dresses. Had she created a false destiny for herself? Always expecting others to let her down, feeling resigned when they did?

She decided to file the revelation away and reexamine later. Nothing so heavy should interfere with Angel's excitement as they shopped.

And such a civilized way to shop, reclined on a comfy overstuffed couch with a glass of champagne, an appreciative audience of one as Angel paraded in and out in a variety of dresses, some long, some short, some traditional, some modern.

"You look terrific no matter what you put on," Montana said much later. By now, she couldn't tell one dress from the other. Obviously she was out of practice at shopping.

"That's because I'm happy," Angel said.

"Not to mention beautiful," Montana said.

"Well, I never expected to be a bride again."

"Any decisions on the dress?"

Angel shook her head. "I have no intention of making a choice so soon. I want to savor the entire experience."

"You don't find this painful? Trying to find the perfect dress?"

"Are you serious? I'm having far too much fun. Come on. It's time to go meet the men for dinner. I'm starving."

Montana hadn't realized just how isolated she'd been out at Black Creek, totally focused on the property. Here in Las Vegas, she felt lighter, younger, and far more carefree than she ever remembered.

Angel and Rake, so happy and easy to be around, ensured that dinner was a lively event with much laughter and friendly banter. She didn't want the evening to end and apparently neither did anyone else, for they all adjourned to the Black Opal Lounge to go dancing.

"They are so happy," Montana mused, watching Angel and Rake on the dance floor, tapping her foot in time to the jazz combo's rendition of "When a Man Loves a Woman."

"We'll see how long it lasts this time," Steele said.

"That's an awful thing to say."

"They've reconciled before. It never lasts."

"They're obviously very much in love."

"Exactly," Steele said. "And how does the song go? Sometimes love ain't enough."

"I figured I'd find you here." Sloan slid into the seat next to Montana and helped himself to a handful of bar munchies. He scanned the dance floor and nodded approvingly. "They look good together."

"Yes," Montana said. "I was just trying to explain to your brother that they're happy and deserve to bask in it. He's a tad cynical."

"Cynical? Steele? Surely you jest."

"Ask Sloan why he hasn't fallen victim to the grand passion," Steele said.

"I haven't met my soul mate yet. When I do, guarantee I won't be running scared."

Steele scowled. "Soul mate? You sound like you actually believe that."

"Why not?" Sloan turned to Montana. "Do you like to dance?"

"I love to dance."

"Then why are we sitting here?"

They joined Rake and Angel and a few other couples on the spacious dance floor. Sloan was an accomplished dancer, easy to follow as he swung her through a series of complicated maneuvers—it felt as if she instinctively knew every move in advance. It was the type of synchronicity that doesn't happen often, and she lost track of how many songs they danced to before the band slowed their tempo to another romantic slow dance, "Can't Help Falling in Love."

Before she could ease into Sloan's waiting arms, Steele elbowed his brother out of the way. With a knowing grin, Sloan retreated gracefully.

"That wasn't very nice." Face-to-face with Steele, she slid

one arm around his neck and placed her hand in his, aware of the possessive way he cinched his arm around her waist, holding her closer than the dance warranted.

"I wasn't feeling nice."

"You could have said 'please.'"

"Next time."

If she'd thought she and Sloan moved well together, it paled to the way her body meshed with Steele's. "You and Sloan are both very good dancers."

"Had to keep up the Hardt tradition: Whatever you do, do it well."

Montana rested her head on his shoulder. "Is there anything you can't do?"

"I haven't found it yet."

Coming from anyone else, such a statement would have sounded conceited, but Steele stated it matter-of-factly.

One song blended into another seamlessly. The tempo increased, but Steele showed no inclination to release her.

She was aware of the muffled beat of his heart against hers, the heat of his skin, his own particular musky smell, and felt herself respond on all levels. Pheromones, maybe. They were both fully clothed, in plain sight of everyone, yet intimately connected in far more ways than merely the physical. Was it as obvious to anyone else as it was to her? The music seeped through her the same way Steele did till she felt saturated, consumed by him.

Twinkling lights added to the air of unreality, enhanced by the headiness of Steele's arms around her. She knew how Cinderella must have felt at the ball.

"Having a good time?" Steele asked.

"I don't want this night to end," she said with a wistful sigh.

"Who says it has to?"

If only she could believe that. "I think I'm ingrained to expect something bad to happen. Things can't possibly stay this good."

"How about if I promise not to let anything bad happen?"

"Can you keep that promise?"

"I told you, I'm good at everything I do."

Montana floated out of the elevator behind Steele, the last bars of their last dance song still running through her mind.

This must be a tiny taste of the "normal" life she never had—with a family, roots, and a sense of belonging in the community. And although she knew she needed to create it for herself in her own community, for now it was lovely to coattail on Steele.

She danced into the bedroom, kicking off her shoes as she went, and flopped onto the bed. Steele loomed over her, frowning.

"How much did you have to drink?"

"Not much. Some champagne while we shopped and wine at dinner."

"Did you eat lunch?"

She shook her head from side to side and got a lovely rush of movement, like a merry-go-round.

"Terrific," Steele muttered. "I leave you with my mother and you come back bombed."

"I'm not bombed." She struggled to her feet to prove the point and pushed him away.

"I take it back." He grinned. "You're just happy."

"So happy!" She flung her arms around his neck to emphasize the point, only staggering a little bit.

"I'm glad you're happy." He gently removed her arms from around his neck.

"I love being happy."

Steele nodded. "That's good. Happy is very good." But his look deepened into an almost-frown and she tugged at the corners of his mouth, trying to force a smile.

"Why so glum? You promised not to let anything bad happen. No planes turning into pumpkins."

He laughed at that, picked her up, and spun her around till she was reeling with dizziness; dizzy from happiness.

He fell back onto the bed, pulling her with him.

"Stay happy, Montana. It suits you."

"It does, doesn't it?"

He took pity on her frustrated tugs at his suit and tie as she tried to undress him, and rose to quickly divest himself of his clothes. He was beautiful and she could happily lie there and admire him for hours. Then it became her turn, when he peeled her out of her dress in seconds.

"I like that you're wearing a whole lot less clothes than me," he said.

"We're even now."

"Even better."

Her skin grew warm just from the power of his heated gaze, the admiring way he touched her. She felt she was being molded and reformed, the way a sculptor works a piece of clay, his touch bringing her to life. Reaching a place, a level, she'd never been before.

There was no urgency in his touch, just a warm and encompassing sensation that transcended the physical, as if he were reaching right inside her, touching the very fiber of her being.

Bringing her to life with his love.

It was almost scary, feeling as if she had no power to move unless it came through him to her, and she struggled through the inertia to rise to her knees above him.

"I wondered how long you'd lie there passive," he said.

"How did I do?"

"Better than I thought."

She kissed him, hungry for him, as if she could draw his very essence from him to fill her. As if her happiness had become an insatiable thing that would never feel totally sated.

"Slow down," he murmured against her lips. "We have all night."

"Yes." Was it wrong to wish they had every night?

She pushed the thought away and concentrated on making the most of the time they had. No toys, no props, no role-play, just her and Steele, and the fact that she cared about him more than she wanted to.

"Make love to me," she whispered. It was as close as she let herself come to saying "love me."

He gave her one of those all-seeing looks and she quickly averted her gaze, in case her feelings were as obvious to him as they were to herself.

She was strong. She was independent. She needed no one.

"You excite me." His fingers grazed her all over, his touch at once light yet arousing. "Today in the boardroom. Tonight on the dance floor. I thought about you all day while we were apart."

"Show me."

He positioned himself between her legs, slid inside of her, and went still. It was almost eerie and she knew he felt it, too—a depth of connection, the sense of completion that they each brought the other. Her heart welled up in her throat till she could barely breathe, and it scared her.

He pushed her hair back from her face. "Feel that?"

She nodded tremulously.

"Don't ever forget."

She shook her head, relieved when she felt him start to move. She moved as well, murmuring her pleasure as he withdrew, then plunged back in, gradually increasing the pace of their joining till all else was blotted from mind and she let herself be spiraled into orbit, aware of nothing except the tight way she clung to him. And the fact that she never wanted to let go.

* * *

> What do the famous Black Opal casino and the not-so-famous Black Creek dude ranch have in common? Other than they are currently both being graced by the presence of former exotic dancer Montana?
>
> The real question is, can Midas work his golden magic on a floundering dude ranch wannabe resort managed by the former stripper? Or does Midas's presence signal the final curtain for Ms. Blackstone's new career? Ladies and gentlemen, place your bets.

Steele balled up the paper and buried it before Montana could see it. He needed to get her out of here and back to the ranch before all hell broke loose.

If she was puzzled by his haste to abandon Las Vegas and race back to the ranch, she kept her thoughts to herself till they were in the air.

"I thought I was going to see your mother's shop before we left."

"Change of plans," he said gruffly.

She fell silent, leaning forward in her seat as she watched the desert fall away beneath them. Then she turned to face him.

"I really want to thank you for everything."

"Forget it."

"I'm serious. It's not easy for me to admit I need help, let alone accept it when it's offered."

He dismissed her words. "Next thing I know, you'll be telling me you couldn't have done it without me."

"I doubt I'd go that far."

He didn't care for the eagle-eyed way she watched him. Not that she'd see him give anything away; he'd been playing his hand close for way too long to let that happen.

"I never expected you'd stick around this long. Particularly once I found out who you are."

Neither had he, but he didn't tell her that. "You get used to seeing the job through is all."

"Is something wrong? You seem different today."

The hell he did! "You're imagining it."

"No, I'm not." She sat back, arms folded across her chest.

"What I think happened is that you got what you want. The game is done. On to the next round."

He was framing his response when Montana's cell phone rang. She dug it out of her purse. "Hello, Helen."

A pause. "We're on our way back. Why?"

He could tell by Montana's expression that the news had leaked. "My God. Yes, tell him to wait." She turned to Steele, eyes wide, face white. "Apparently there's a pack of news reporters camped out at the ranch. Along with my main backer, worried about his investment, and Black Creek's future."

She wished Steele didn't have such a poker face. She had no idea what he was thinking and no inclination to ask.

"What can I do?" he said.

"Nothing. This is all my fault."

"How is it your fault?"

"It must have come from the interview I gave that woman from *Spa* magazine. I felt her digging the entire time but I ignored my instincts. She was looking for something, and by God, she found it."

"Why should your former career make any difference to your capabilities today?"

"You and I both know it doesn't, any more than being a gambler discredits you. But I'm disappointed in Melvin. I expected better of him."

Montana spent the remainder of the flight scribbling notes to herself, organizing her thoughts. This was no time to be dwelling on her disappointments. The disappointment that Melvin didn't have enough faith in her to weather out this storm. Disappointment that her past, which she'd thought was well and truly forgotten, still had the power to unsettle the life she'd built at Black Creek. Disappointment with herself for having let down her guard. She'd wanted to believe Steele's promise that nothing bad could happen as long as he was around with his golden touch.

He let her alone, thank goodness, reclined in his seat with his eyes closed. Forget about Steele, she told herself firmly. Focus on reassuring Melvin, so he could reassure the rest of his board.

Helen had sent an ATV for them and they reached the ranch house through back trails, unseen by the reporters out front.

There certainly were a lot of them. Montana was almost flattered that her checkered past had suddenly made her a hot news item. Surely there must be some way to turn all this publicity to her advantage.

Melvin's normally florid face was a brighter red than usual, not a good indicator of his blood pressure.

"It's not my decision, Montana, you know that. I'm speaking for all the investors."

"Their money is as secure as ever, Melvin. You and I both know that."

"Ranching isn't the secure future it once was, no more than dude ranches."

"That's precisely why I'm taking Black Creek in a new direction."

"You're considerably over budget," Melvin pointed out.

"Who knew there would be a building boom, pushing up the price of materials and labor?"

"Someone more experienced, perhaps?"

"Buy me some time, Melvin. I can't stop now, even if I want to, or the entire project goes under."

"Montana. You've run through all Charlie's insurance money, and more than maxed out the line of credit we agreed upon. Everyone knows a new business needs capital to keep it afloat the first couple of years. Where are you planning to get that capital?"

"I'll get it."

"My people have no intention of throwing good money after bad."

"I've got an idea." When Steele spoke up from the other side of the room, Montana swung around. She'd forgotten he was there. In fact, he wouldn't be, if she'd had her way. Melvin had requested that Steele stay, though, and she hadn't wanted to do anything that might spook Melvin.

"You need something to throw the investors, right? Calm them down so they don't call in Montana's loans?"

"And your presence is hardly helping. You being here is a red flag to them that the project needs help," Montana said.

Steele turned to Helen. "Go tell the press that Montana and I are preparing a statement and that we'll be right out."

"No." Vehemence rang through Montana's voice.

He turned to Melvin. "Do you want to tell her, or shall I?"

"Tell me what?" Her gaze flew from one man to the other. She raised her voice. "Tell me *what?*"

"Helen didn't hire me to come in here, Montana. Melvin did."

"*What?* You sent Steele in here, incognito, to check up on me?"

"The investors were getting skittish. The thumbs-up from Steele would buy you the time you needed."

She turned to Steele. "Have you filed your report yet?"

He nodded.

"Do I get a copy?"

"Take it up with Melvin. He paid for it."

She turned to Helen. Her mother-in-law stood wringing her hands, avoiding her eyes. "You were in on this?"

"Not exactly, dear. I just wanted what was best for everyone."

"And now Midas is going to make it all better with his golden touch. Is that how it works?"

Steele gave her a long, challenging look. "Are you holding or folding? 'Cause if you're holding, you're walking through those doors with me and facing the press."

"I'll never fold."

She stomped from the room and down the hall, where she flung open the front doors, Steele on her heels.

A barrage of shouted questions greeted her, microphones shoved near as cameras flashed. A TV camera nearly blinded her with its light. She opened her mouth, then realized she didn't have a clue what to say.

Steele, however, suffered from no such malaise.

"Thank you, everyone, for your patience and for giving Montana and me this chance to set the record straight."

"Can your golden touch salvage the Black Creek project?"

Steele squeezed her waist. When had he slipped his arm around her? Montana felt herself recede into the background, retreating into her safe-on-stage persona. She couldn't see these people. They didn't really exist except en masse. She had no need to interact with them.

"The truth is, I'm not here in any official capacity. Black Creek is not now, nor ever was, on any sort of shaky ground."

"Right," drawled a cynical female voice. "So what are you doing here?"

"I would have thought that was obvious. Montana and I met and fell in love. That's why we flew out to Vegas. I wanted my parents to meet their future daughter-in-law."

There was a collective murmur as reporters scribbled in their notebooks and cameras flashed and clicked.

Great, Montana thought. What else was he going to say?

"How do your parents feel about having a stripper in the family?"

She blanched, even though she ought to have been expecting that one.

Steele laughed. "My mother danced on the Vegas stage for more years than I've kept track of. My folks are both thrilled."

"Have you set a date yet?"

He pulled her close and pressed a kiss to her forehead. "Well, I've been pushing her, but Montana won't give me an answer till after the resort and spa are open for business."

"When will that be?"

"The grand opening's next week. And we look forward to seeing all of you here for the festivities."

"You must feel like the luckiest woman on earth, Montana."

Steele gave her an encouraging squeeze and she stepped forward. "You know the old saying: the harder you work, the luckier you get."

With a smile, she turned and went back into the house, walking past those gathered inside. When she reached the doorway to her office, she turned to face them.

"I'd appreciate it if you'd all leave my home."

"Who's for coffee?" Zeb asked, as he, Helen, Steele, and Melvin settled around the scarred wooden table in the bunkhouse kitchen.

"Got anything stronger?" Melvin mopped his face with his handkerchief.

Zeb fetched a bottle of whiskey and glasses. Steele opened the fridge and helped himself to a beer.

"Now what happens?" Helen asked.

Steele popped the top of the bottle and took a long swallow. "Montana's a pro. The show must go on, and she knows it."

"And the press?"

"We couldn't have planned a better PR splash for the grand opening. Everyone's happy, right, Melvin?"

"I'll make 'em happy," Melvin said.

"You two certainly seem happy." Steele transferred his gaze to Helen and Zeb.

Helen blushed like a schoolgirl. Zeb harrumphed and ran a finger around the inside of his shirt collar.

"I thought you were too involved with Montana to notice anybody else."

Steele forced a laugh. "Don't take what I said at the press release seriously. That was a PR stunt."

Melvin perked right up. "Why not? I can see you and Montana making a match."

"Hardly a match," Steele said. "We're both way too independent."

Helen smiled and squeezed Zeb's knee. "That's what we both thought, didn't we?"

Steele was surprised to see the old cowpoke light up like a Christmas tree.

"As soon as things are settled here, Miss Helen and I are lighting out."

"Lighting out where?" Steele said. "Montana needs you."

"You get to be our age and you realize you need to do for you."

"You sound like my parents."

Melvin stood and hitched his pants. "I guess I'll be heading back to the city. Steele, looks like it's up to you."

He frowned. "What's up to me? My work here is finished."

"You can't leave. It'll give more fodder to the press."

"Montana won't appreciate me staying."

"Montana doesn't know what she wants."

Montana knew exactly what she wanted. And Sloan Hardt was just the one to give it to her.

She found him exactly where she expected, in the stables.

If Steele was a chameleon, easily adapting himself to his surroundings, Sloan was the genuine article. What you saw was what you got.

"Take a ride with me?" she asked.

If Sloan was surprised by her offer, he hid it well. "Sure thing."

"You look like you get mighty itchy if you're out of a saddle for too long."

Sloan laughed. "Don't think you can pigeonhole a Hardt. We'll surprise you every time."

"So I'm learning."

They saddled up and headed east.

"It's quite the spread," Sloan said. "They don't make them like this anymore."

"My late husband fancied himself a gentleman rancher, more at home in a fast plane or a fast car than in a saddle. But Black Creek always deserved more. Someone with passion for the land."

"And now it has you."

Montana fell silent. She'd never thought of herself as a passionate person.

"I have a different vision for the place. But it's limited, and I'm smart enough to know that."

"Why do I get the feeling you have an ulterior motive for bringing me out here?"

"I see now that I've been going about this all wrong. My energies and my focus have been diluted, as I try to divide myself in too many directions. No wonder my backers are feeling nervous."

"Steele will take care of them. It's what he does."

"Steele is easily bored. It occurred to me I don't need a foreman, I need a partner. Someone to take over the ranch side of the operation so I can concentrate on the resort."

"Is this going where I think it's going?"

"Steele said you were looking for new challenges."

Sloan laughed. "I didn't think he noticed."

"At least think about it, Sloan. We'll put it together any way you want. Long-term lease. Option-to-buy clause."

They stopped on a slight rise, with the Black Creek vista in every direction.

"Strikes me this would make a pretty decent building site," he said slowly.

Montana smiled. "It's a perfect building site."

The next week was an insane blur of activity as the newly hired staff arrived to be housed, oriented, and uniformed. Temperaments clashed and misunderstandings were smoothed over. Publicity snowballed and the phone rang off the hook. The resort was filling up nicely, the spa was in full operation, and nearly all was ready for the grand opening bash on the weekend.

As much as Montana hated to admit it, Steele was proving to be a godsend. Not only did he know exactly how she wanted things done, often before she did, but people listened to him and followed his directives.

She couldn't bear to be anywhere near him. His presence was a reminder of her vulnerability, the way she'd let her guard drop in Las Vegas. Ever since their return to Black Creek, she'd worked frantically to resurrect those buffers between herself and the rest of the world.

At the moment, she was hiding in her office, going over last-minute checklists for Saturday's festivities.

Helen poked her head in. "Montana, could I speak with you a moment, please?"

"Can it possibly wait, Helen? I'm up to my ears here."

Mercifully, her mother-in-law retreated. Montana rolled her aching shoulders, aware it was high time she took advantage of having several massage therapists on the payroll.

Working this hard was good therapy. It prevented her from thinking too much about anything else, even as she silenced the tiny voice inside that asked what she planned to do when she no longer had the work distraction.

Lawyers were drawing up the long-term lease agreement between Black Creek Ranch and Sloan Hardt. She had no idea what Steele thought of the idea and told herself she didn't care. But apparently she was about to find out, for there he stood, filling the doorway, larger than life. The sight of him gave her such a rush of adrenaline, she literally felt dizzy.

"Okay. I've left you alone to stew in your own juices long enough. It's time you pulled your head out of the sand and took a look around you."

"Get out of my office, Steele."

Of course he did the exact opposite, dwarfing the room

with his presence as he made his way to her side. "Not a chance, doll. Not until you hear me out. It's my reputation on the line here. My word that this project is solid."

"I should have figured that's all you were worried about."

"It's an improvement over you, who's oblivious to everything and everyone around you."

"I resent that."

"Poor Helen has been trying to get your attention long enough to tell you that she and Zeb are in love and planning to elope."

"What?" Montana half stood, then flopped back down into her chair. "Why didn't she tell me?"

"Apparently every time she tries to talk to you, you brush her aside like some pesky fly. Zeb, too. If you took a minute to actually look, you'd see it sticking out all over them. You wouldn't need a formal announcement."

Montana squashed her guilt. She *had* been self-involved, trying to lose all memory of the woman she'd been in Vegas. It wasn't comfortable out there, unguarded and vulnerable.

Unfortunately the old groove wasn't comfortable, either, which left her defensive and on edge. Especially around Steele.

"Speaking of formal announcements, when are you breaking off our fake engagement?"

"I'll let you deal with that any way you want."

"Fine. I'll leak it at the spa's grand opening. Lots of press will be around." She cleared her throat. "It would be helpful if you weren't there."

He gave her a long, hard look, which she did her best to avoid. "So the jilted fiancée can play to the press?"

He saw through her like glass, damn him. She blew out a frustrated breath. "Melvin hired you to check the place over, in and out without a ripple. Why are you still hanging around?"

"Could be I enjoy pissing you off."

"You give yourself far too much credit. I barely even notice you."

He advanced. "Now *my* feelings are hurt. After all I've done, and this is my thanks? Turfed on my ear. Denied the tiniest crumb of your moment of triumph."

He knew how to take the wind from her sails, fast. "You predict there'll be a triumph?"

"If I was a gambling man, I'd put money on it."

"What happened to 'once a gambler, always a gambler'?"

"I'm reformed." As always, those intense blue eyes saw everything and gave away nothing. "Your lease idea was sheer brilliance. Sloan was restless, and Gramps is acting decades younger now that the reins have been tossed back to him."

She'd expected him to be cynical and sarcastic, not complimentary. She hated it when people didn't behave as expected.

The telephone rang and Montana felt a surge of relief. "It never stops."

Helen stuck her head in the door. "Sorry to interrupt, but you'll want to take this call."

Montana shot a glance at Steele, but he showed no sign of budging as she picked up the receiver. "Montana Blackstone . . . Really? . . . What an honor . . . Well, of course I'll be there. I wouldn't miss it. What time would you like me?"

She scribbled the details on the pad in front of her, then put down the phone in a daze.

Steele lounged against her desk, arms folded over his chest. "Good news?"

"The local chamber of commerce has voted me entrepreneur of the year. There's a luncheon Saturday and they've asked me there to accept the award."

"Same day as the grand opening?"

"I should make it back in plenty of time."

"Congratulations," Steele said shortly. "Looks like you've got everything you want."

After Steele left, Montana sat there in a state of numbness. It might look like she had everything she wanted, so why didn't it feel that way? She should jump up and share her happy news, but there was no one to share it with. She'd done too good a job protecting her solitude.

Memory fragments flashed before her. Her parents were such a tight couple, she always felt like an outsider. Then her mother's rebound marriage, reinforcing that Montana would never be enough. Duke in her life, then alone again till she met Charlie and entered another world she never quite fit into.

Could it have been her all this time, pushing people away? Never allowing anyone close, afraid of needing someone as desperately as her mother did? She went looking for Helen. They'd never been close, but maybe it wasn't too late.

She found her mother-in-law curled up on the porch swing with Zeb, the two of them engrossed in such a private, intimate moment, she couldn't intrude. Steele was right. One look at them was all it took to see the glow of love and affection cocooning them in a visible aura. How could she have been so blind?

She backed away before they saw her.

A plane's engine droned overhead and she looked up to see an aircraft shrinking in the distance. She'd asked Steele to leave. It appeared he'd taken her at her word.

Everything was under control. The resort was booked up beyond her wildest expectations. So why was she feeling so let down now that she'd realized her dream? Or had she let herself down, chasing a false dream?

Her triumph felt as empty and as hollow as her life; she needed something and had no idea what it was.

It wasn't about fame. It wasn't about fortune. It wasn't even about the recognition she was about to receive on Saturday.

She made her way through the hive of activity at the resort, where the staff members greeted her by name. The noise and bustle was overwhelming, the drone of worker bees in their hive. The hive she'd created was so full, yet so empty at the same time.

Deep in thought, she made her way to the place where the creek widened out. On their first anniversary, Charlie had shipped in a load of sand to create her own private beach, complete with bright plastic sand toys, joking that his child-bride needed someplace to play. She hadn't appreciated till this moment that maybe Charlie knew her better than she knew herself, recognizing what she needed and giving her permission to play.

She'd come to love the spot, her own private retreat. Few people knew of its existence, and those who did knew enough to stay away. But with the resort set to open, it was time to say good-bye to a special place that had been both a haven and an albatross, a reminder of the solitude of her life.

A weeping willow grew near the shore, its branches a curtain between herself and the rest of the world. She plucked an end off one soft branch and crushed the bright green leaves between her fingers. The scent of life renewed. What did she have to do to renew hers?

"I wasn't sure if you planned on swimming or sulking. But either way, I figured you ought to be celebrating."

She spun around. Steele tossed her a towel and pulled a bottle of champagne and two glasses from his pack.

"I'm not sure I deserve to celebrate."

"I was right about the sulking, then."

"Don't be silly. I have everything I've ever dreamed of."

"Dreams don't always make sense." His words were echoed by the loud pop of the cork.

"I saw the plane leave. I thought you were on it."

He placed a glass of champagne in her hand. "Think you can get rid of me so easy?"

"I figured I'd alienated you, along with everyone else in my life."

"You're doing a good job."

Was it her imagination, or was he trying a little too hard with the heart-of-steel act? It hadn't been all about her in Las Vegas; there had been two of them. Maybe her man of steel wasn't quite as bulletproof as he made himself out to be.

With Sloan running the ranch, Steele would be around from time to time. Better they learn to be civil. She slugged back her champagne in a single, unladylike swallow.

"You didn't let me make a toast."

She held out her glass for a refill. "Ever think maybe I didn't want to hear what you'd have to say?"

"Pretty much every time I open my mouth."

"Which doesn't do much to dissuade you, does it?"

"Nope. We both know I showed you up for the fraud that you are, not-so-tough lady."

He stood far too close and Montana retaliated by sinking to a sitting position on the sand. Too late she realized what a mistake that had been, for he followed suit, closer than ever.

She had to get away!

She ripped off her shoes and socks. "Skinny-dipping—I dare you. Last one in is a rotten egg!"

She didn't for a second think he'd take the dare, and she was right. He stayed put, watching her every move as she stood and dropped her clothes in a pile. He'd seen her naked before; a body was just a body, something she'd learned back in her dancing days.

The creek water was cold. Maybe it would shock some sense back into her befuddled brain.

She floated on her back, staring up at the sky for answers that didn't exist, as the water caressed her limbs in sensory pleasure. How long had it been since she'd skinny-dipped?

She unexpectedly felt his arm around her waist, like a coiling snake. She flailed in a blur of panicked motion, but too late, for he had her in his clutches.

"Steele, I—"

"I always was a rotten egg." He kissed her long and hard, and she melted against him.

She wanted him.

She needed him.

And as scary as her need was, her want was greater.

She tried to beat a hasty retreat away from her needs and fears, but they followed her everywhere, lodged deep inside, choking her, drowning her.

The harder she struggled, the more all-consuming her fears were. Did she struggle against herself, or against Steele?

She thrashed, sucking in a mouthful of water, coughing and sputtering as she struggled, feeling unseen forces suck her down below the surface and hold her there.

As strong arms pulled her to the surface, she coughed, sucked in lungfuls of air, and found herself tossed unceremoniously onto shore.

"What the hell was that all about?" Steele faced her, breathing heavily, magnificently male. She craved his strength even as she knew it would weaken her, the way too much heat softened glue till it no longer held.

She and Steele generated too much heat to ever be effective together.

"I don't know." She coughed again and drew a deep, shuddery breath. "All of a sudden it was like lead weights were attached to my legs and arms, dragging me down."

"Maybe you ought to try not carrying the whole burden. Let people help you when they can."

"I think that's the problem. I did let you help."

"And that freaks you out so much, you feel compelled to push me away."

"It's the only way I know how to survive."

"You can learn a new way."

She reached for him. "Show me."

"You can't do this, Montana."

"Can't do what?"

"Use sex the way other people use alcohol or drugs to deaden the pain."

"Damn you, I don't want to feel dead. I want to feel alive." She struggled to her feet and wound her arms around his neck. "Bring me to life."

"Damn *you!* I keep going all in with you, and I keep losing. Yet I keep going back for more."

"Steele, I'm all in, too."

"You don't have a clue about all in. And I don't know when the hell to sit out my hand."

He covered her mouth with his, his breath filling the emptiness. She felt suddenly light, free of all burdens, like a helium balloon let loose toward the heavens, and clung to him, trusting him to anchor her.

"Mouth-to-mouth," he said huskily. "Bringing you back to life."

"I shouldn't need or want you this much," she moaned.

"You don't. Not nearly as much as I want you."

What the hell came over him, making such an admission? But it must have been the right thing to say, for she drooped against him, so limp he scooped her into his arms and carried her to the towel.

Her skin was cool from the creek and he warmed her inch by inch, feeling her temperature rise and her body's response as he kissed and licked and suckled every inch of her. She lay pliant beneath him, as if he were the sun and she the dormant seed germinating and poking its head through the soil. Slowly she began to move, her arms clutching him, her legs rubbing against him. Her lips accepted his kiss, doubling and trebling the sweetness. He set the pace and she followed, moving in sweet synchronicity as he thrust and parried, taking them to a whirlwind of orgasmic bliss that carried them to the outer universe.

Chapter Sixteen

Montana wriggled in her seat and glanced at her watch, wondering how much longer before she could make her escape. The chamber luncheon and awards ceremony had been as dry and long-winded as she had expected, pulling in nearly a hundred local business owners to eat rubber chicken and discuss the long-term goals of the community.

Despite the fact she wrote a check every year and skimmed through the newsletter when it arrived, this was the first time she'd actually attended a meeting. Yet everyone knew who she was and seemed genuine in their congratulations.

As the president droned on, Montana snuck another peek at her watch, wondering how things were faring at the resort. Perhaps she could head for the washroom and forget to come back.

Then she heard her name. Suddenly people were looking her way and nodding; a few even clapped. She gave a tentative nod and smile. Too late she realized she'd just accepted the nomination to run for the upcoming year's executive board.

And glancing around the room, she realized maybe it wasn't such a bad thing to get more involved. Hadn't she been alone long enough?

"You know, bro, I don't know the lady very well, but I predict Montana is going to flip out when she sees this."

"Maybe at first. But once she gets used to the idea, she'll realize it was a good one. Maybe even start to think it was hers."

Sloan pulled back and gave his brother a long, searching look. "Man, you have it bad."

"I don't know what you're talking about." Steele flashed a thumbs-up to the driver of the grader.

"Do me a favor: If I ever fall in love, shake some sense into me, would you? 'Cause I don't ever want to find myself in the same sorry state as you. It's bad enough our parents have turned into lovesick teenagers. I didn't expect to ever see it happen to you."

Steele shrugged. "I gambled. I lost. I should have told her who I was up front."

"Hardts never accept defeat. Not when there's always another hand being dealt."

"True. But I've never had to lay all my cards faceup, either."

Montana drove home from the luncheon with the trophy buckled into the seat beside her. It was hers till next year when it got passed on to the next up-and-coming entrepreneur, with her doing the honors.

It looked like someone was doing roadwork up ahead, for she passed a large-scale grader and excavator as she turned onto the road to Black Creek. It was a perfect day for the grand opening: not too hot nor too cold, a flawless blue sky decorated with a few cotton-candy wisps of cloud. As long as enough people actually showed up.

Only after she trundled across the wooden bridge over Black Creek did she slow her vehicle to a crawl.

She'd been so deep in thought, she totally missed the spa driveway! Rather than turn around, she decided to take the old driveway to the ranch, which looped past the ranch house and came out in back of the spa.

After a short distance she slammed on the brakes and stared at a brand-new driveway, bannered with a welcome sign to Black Creek Resort and Ranch.

She released the brake and turned onto the smooth, graded expanse, liking what she saw. They'd need to plant trees on either side, of course, something leafy and elegant to make the guests feel relaxed and welcomed.

A short distance later the new driveway forked, and attractive logoed signs directed her to the Black Creek Ranch to the east and the Black Creek Resort and Spa to the west. In the middle, like the jewel in the crown, sat the ranch house.

Home.

Somehow it had never looked more welcoming.

She headed for the spa, up a driveway lined with bright-colored flags that fluttered in the breeze. The parking lot was already clogged with cars and it wasn't even three o'clock.

As she got out of the car, Chef waved to her from behind his huge, shiny stainless steel barbeque. Not far from the food station, Helen and Zeb served beer, wine, and punch at a portable bar. A five-piece band on a bandstand played toned-down classic rock music. Tables and chairs, shaded from the sun by brightly colored umbrellas, stood ready and waiting as guests mingled about, eating, drinking, and signing up for tours of the resort and spa.

It was her dream, only so much more—as if black and white had become Technicolor. She felt like Alice not yet in Wonderland: still on the outside looking in, aware that it was time to take the plunge, to step through the looking glass into the rest of her life.

She started by approaching the bar. A glass of wine definitely seemed in order.

"Montana. How was the luncheon? As bad as you thought?"

She'd never seen Helen look so radiant. Zeb, at her side, was spit and polished in a Western shirt with a string tie and a new Stetson.

"Not at all," she said. "I agreed to run for the board."

"Great idea," Helen said. "You need to get more involved in the community."

"That's what I thought."

She next headed to the barbeque, relieved to see Daniel and Bradley working together like old friends.

Bradley waved a pair of barbeque tongs in greeting. "Nothing like combining the best of the old and the new, Montana. Hot dogs and chili."

"Paired with pork tenderloin crostinis, rhubarb compote, and endive salad."

"Good thing you two talked me out of hiring a caterer."

"Too many cooks spoil the broth," Bradley said. "Isn't that right, Daniel?"

The party continued on around her as a clown blew up balloons for the kids, jugglers juggled, and a magician performed her tricks. The spa director organized guests into groups for the tour.

At exactly three o'clock, as prearranged, the band stopped playing. Into the sudden silence came a crash of cymbals, followed by a drum roll, as Montana handed the mayor an oversized pair of scissors to cut the bright red ribbon draped across the doorway.

He proclaimed, "I now declare the Black Creek Resort and Spa officially open."

There was a hearty round of applause, and the band members picked up their instruments and started to play. In the midst of the commotion, Montana fielded several press interviews and posed with her new trophy.

"Montana, we noticed the brand-new driveway. Could you fill us in on the significance of the newly designed approach?"

"Actually, the driveway was a total surprise to me."

"Are you saying you weren't consulted? Aren't you angry about that?"

"Not at all. The Black Creek project is a joint effort, with a great many people working behind the scenes to pull it all together. And I have total trust in my people."

"You never used to be a team player, Montana. Don't tell us you're mellowing," Murdoch's voice taunted.

She saw him at the back of the crowd. "I've learned a lot recently."

"I'm surprised you invited him," said a nearby female reporter, her words for Montana's ears alone.

"Why wouldn't I?"

The woman shrugged. "Everyone knows he's the one who tried to drag your reputation through the mud and destroy your credibility by leaking all that exotic dancer stuff."

"Murdoch did that?"

The reporter nodded. "He's got a reputation for playing dirty. Where's that handsome fiancé of yours?"

"Steele is . . . ah . . ."

This was her chance to announce she that and Steele had parted ways, but her throat closed down. She couldn't force the words out. She didn't *want* to force the words out. She wanted Steele in her present and her future, not her past.

"I'm right here."

Like something from her dreams, her man stepped forward and the day suddenly got a whole lot brighter. Steele was here. She wasn't alone.

Montana moved toward him and wrapped her arms around him as if it was the most natural thing in the world. "I missed you. I love the driveway! What a wonderful surprise!"

She gestured toward the waiting reporter and said to Steele, "Now tell the story."

"There's not much to tell. This is no easy lady to surprise."

"But the idea came from somewhere," the reporter said.

"It struck me that sometimes we get locked into thinking that we're involved in an all-or-nothing deal, when it doesn't have to be that way at all. Black Creek Resort can be its own independent entity, and still be part of Black Creek Ranch."

"So Montana will run the resort and you'll run the ranch?"

"Actually, my brother Sloan is the ranch guy."

"Then what will your role be in this venture?"

"I'm sure there will always be some venture that requires my golden touch."

The reporter turned to face the camera. "There you have it, folks. Looks like another winning hand for this retired gambler and his lady. Coming to you live from Black Creek Resort, Oregon, this is Frannie Hingle for CJOV."

The local newspaper journalist lobbied for his turn. "Is it true we're looking at a wedding? Which black widow is set to tie the knot?"

Montana shook her head. "I have no idea what Helen's up to." She turned to Steele. "Do you?"

"A little bit. Here she is now."

Helen appeared clutching two wedding bouquets. She hugged Montana and passed her the smaller one. "I need a maid of honor."

Montana stared at the flowers. "What's this all about?"

"Zeb and I thought, as long as everyone was already here and set to party, we might as well make it official."

"Helen! Are you sure?"

Helen pulled her close. "It was all Zeb's idea. It was the one way he could think of to make sure Steele didn't leave."

Montana glanced over at Steele, standing near Zeb and a woman carrying a Bible. Did he still want to leave? Was he just here today to help her save face?

"I don't believe you two," Montana said, and let herself be dragged by Helen to where the others waited.

Abruptly, the band broke into a jazzy rendition of "Here Comes the Bride." When the hubbub died down, Helen and Zeb, beaming with happiness, exchanged brief vows they'd written themselves and were declared husband and wife.

The crowd cheered, champagne corks flew, and the party really got started. The dance floor was packed with people, familiar faces mixed in with the newcomers, including Angel and Rake. Sloan grabbed Montana away from a neighboring rancher for a dance, and Montana wondered how she had ever expected she could thrive on her own.

She finally managed a quiet minute to make a long-overdue phone call back at the house. "Mom. I just wanted you to know that I miss you. And as soon as you can get away, I want you to come visit me at the ranch . . . Yes, we're in the midst of our grand opening . . . I wish you were here . . . I love you, too."

Montana put down the phone and turned to see Steele watching her.

"You told your mother you love her."

Montana blinked back a lone tear. "I don't know why that took me so long. Three little words."

"They're not always that easy to say."

She took a step forward. Could she say them again? "Why is that, do you suppose?"

"Lots of reasons."

"You told me once that sometimes love isn't enough."

"Well, wasn't I the cynical idiot? Who'd ever listen to me?"

With a burst of laughter, she flew into his arms. This time she knew for sure he'd always be there to catch her.

"I love you, Steele, you and your golden touch. It's magic, what you pulled off here today."

"I love you, too. And I hardly deserve all the credit. Everyone pitched in."

"Still, it was truly a grand opening bash no other business will ever be able to top."

"And you didn't mind sharing the limelight with Helen and Zeb?"

"Funny, I'm learning that I love to share. Share the work, share the credit, share the fun."

"What else are you learning to share?" He was suddenly serious.

She tilted her head so she could meet his gaze. "Sharing my life."

"You sure?"

"I've never been more sure. But there's just one thing."

"What's that?"

"You need to propose to me officially, not some mocked-up PR stunt."

He blew out his breath. "That was the biggest gamble of my life. One I would have hated to lose."

"I don't think you're programmed to lose."

"You had me worried for a time there."

"Not as much as you had *me* scared. It took me until now to realize just how empty my life had been. Today I realized how satisfying it is to become involved, to feel that connection to others."

"Do you think the guests could handle another wedding bash soon?"

"I'm sure they'd love it. And who knows? Maybe Black Creek will become famous as a wedding resort."

"That's a great idea. I can just see the headlines now."

As she warmed to Steele's kiss, Montana melted into him, secure in the knowledge that going all in had its rewards. Especially when you took home the grandest prize of all.